As another it's time to ma swirling rumor ballroom shadows as together we name the 1813

Society's Most Scandalous

The winner of the *ton*'s most dishonorable accolade will be published on the morning after the final ball of the season. With the infamous Fitzroys' twin daughters and niece making their long-awaited debuts, we can't wait to discover what scandal awaits!

Read Hattie Fitzroy's story in
How to Woo a Wallflower by Virginia Heath

Kitty Fitzroy's story in
How to Cheat the Marriage Mart by Millie Adams

And look for Annie Fitzroy's story in
How to Survive a Scandal by Christine Merrill
Coming soon!

MILLIE ADAMS

—

How to Cheat the Marriage Mart

Special thanks and acknowledgment are given
to Millie Adams for her contribution to the
Society's Most Scandalous collection.

Recycling programs
for this product may
not exist in your area.

ISBN-13: 978-1-335-72341-3

How to Cheat the Marriage Mart

Copyright © 2022 by Harlequin Enterprises ULC

For questions and comments about the quality of this book,
please contact us at CustomerService@Harlequin.com.

Harlequin Enterprises ULC
22 Adelaide St. West, 41st Floor
Toronto, Ontario M5H 4E3, Canada
www.Harlequin.com

Printed in U.S.A.

Millie Adams has always loved books. She considers herself a mix of Anne Shirley (loquacious but charming and willing to break a slate over a boy's head if need be) and Charlotte Doyle (a lady at heart, but with the spirit to become a mutineer should the occasion arise). Millie lives in a small house on the edge of the woods, which she finds allows her to escape in the way she loves best—in the pages of a book. She loves intense alpha heroes and the women who dare to go toe-to-toe with them (or break a slate over their heads).

Books by Millie Adams

Harlequin Historical

Claimed for the Highlander's Revenge
Marriage Deal with the Devilish Duke
The Duke's Forbidden Ward

Society's Most Scandalous

How to Cheat the Marriage Mart

Visit the Author Profile page
at Harlequin.com.

Prologue

15th June 1813

My dear Lords, Ladies and Gentlemen of the ton,
*While the marriage of Lady Harriet Fitzroy to the
Earl of Beaufort has created a storm indeed, it
has not distracted us from the pursuit of naming*
Society's Most Scandalous.

*It seems that, as usual, George Claremont, the
Marquess of Curran, is working to take the hal-
lowed Claremont name and make it ever more
associated with his many and various impropri-
eties! This Season has seen him sneaking out of
nearly every ball he's attended before the evening has ended. It appears he is associating with
women in scarlet in the streets, while hunting for
a wife at the fêtes!*

*Will Lord Curran be the one to seize the title
of* Society's Most Scandalous? *Only time and further misconduct will tell.*
Yours ever in scandal,
The Times *Society Editors*

Chapter One

Miss Katherine Fitzroy—only ever called Kitty—had become a connoisseur of an excellent corner.

A *good* corner—in her estimation—was somewhat spacious, and yet just tight enough that no one would be tempted to join her in it. An excellent corner would accommodate those needs, and might also boast the tail end of an elaborately painted fresco that would give her something to muse on as she stood there avoiding social interaction.

Her consternation at discovering tonight's ballroom was perfectly egg-shaped had been without measure.

There was no easy corner to tuck herself into. Not a single alcove or cranny to be found in the entire ballroom. It was smooth.

And yes, she could find a space upon the wall in which to situate her figure, but it was not as decisive as a corner.

Her nose twitched as she found herself wedged into the rounded bottom of the ballroom egg, and looked around.

She did not wish to be approached.

Not for dancing nor conversation.

The London Season had been difficult on her. It was not within the bounds of her comfort. She had moved to London after the death of her father two years prior, but she had managed to stay more or less secreted away in the family home of the Fitzroys, too young to make her debut in society. It had given her a hard shove away from her quiet, country life, where she had known nothing but endless days of reading, riding horses and wandering about in the mud.

And grief. There had been grief there. Here…it was busy.

London was filled with sights and smells and sounds. It was vibrant and exciting on the surface and there had been a moment when she'd allowed it to captivate her. But the longer she remained, what had become most notable to her was not the aristocracy and all that glittered, but the egregious inequalities. Here in the city she had been confronted with vast poverty—true unsolvable poverty—for the first time in her life.

It wasn't as if there were not poor people in the village where she had grown up. She herself had certainly not been accounted for among the wealthy. But they took care of their poor. They brought them breakfast. Baskets full of food. Blankets. And while there was certainly a show of that made about the city, the poor vastly outnumbered the rich. And for the most part, they were simply left to their own devices, which were lacking at best.

She sighed heavily and reached into her reticule.

Her knitting was in there. She was working on a pair of socks.

Socks. Of all the paltry, inane works.

She knew that the Duchess of Avondale, her aunt, patroness and guardian, meant well, having her knitting circles and fashioning socks for the children at the hospital.

It was an introduction to philanthropy, and Kitty supposed that she shouldn't be disdainful of it. Kitty's cousin Hattie—though she was married now, and enjoying her new life—was deeply enmeshed in the cause of the hospital, and had got her mother to champion it—to an extent. Anne, her other cousin, Hattie's twin, was still at home, the same as Kitty, and they had all supported Hattie in this cause.

It had been pointed out to the Duchess on many occasions that rather than financing a lavish luncheon to get ladies to come and knit socks, she could simply make a donation to the hospital. But she did not seem to understand that point. No matter how many times it was raised.

And so Kitty knitted socks. She knitted them obsessively. She knitted them while she thought long and hard about every atrocity in the world.

She knitted them while she pondered the absurdity of knitting a pair of socks for a child who only had one foot, maimed as he had been in a factory accident. A factory accident. *Children* should not be working in *factories*.

Another egregious thing that ate endlessly at Kitty.

Another problem with all of these events was that

people wanted to speak of *fashion*. They wanted to talk about gossip in the *ton*. They were competing for the title of society's most scandalous, something that George Claremont, Marquess of Curran, seemed hell-bent on having as his own.

It was all so shallow. So *pointless*.

And Lord Curran was perhaps the most pointless of them all.

He was a *Claremont*. He had access to the political in ways that few people did. A marquess, heir to the duchy, and what did he do? He swanned about ball-rooms drinking, looking far too handsome for his own good in clothing—a single outfit—the cost of which could feed an entire family for a year. His boots could be sold to fund an *orphanage*.

But there he was, swanning about. All pomp and very little circumstance.

She huffed, her needles working diligently as she worked her way through the ribbing on the tiny sock. The yarn ball was safely ensconced in her reticule, and she hunched slightly to conceal what she was doing.

On principle, she had asked to wear one of Hattie's discarded gowns to the ball tonight. The Duchess had been in a state about it, but Hattie had stood for Kitty's principles, which Kitty very much appreciated.

She tried very hard to stick to her growing principles even while she was being made to fit in this mould of society.

She had no choice. And she knew it.

She had to marry, else she had no idea what would become of her. The Duke and Duchess's charity towards her could not be endless. She was one of those poor relations. Her father had given up everything to be with her mother. He'd had little money. He'd been committed to charity as well, and Kitty applauded him for it. But she'd been left without a dowry. It was the Duke and Duchess of Avondale who were providing that for her. It was the Duke and Duchess giving her a chance to make a life for herself.

Kitty liked to believe she was practical. There was a way the world should be, and there was a way it was. That a woman in her position had to marry in order to survive was simply the order of things, but that did not mean she could look forward to it. To going from being under the care of her father, to her aunt and uncle, and eventually to a man who would be a near stranger. A man she would call husband.

The very idea made everything inside of her rebel. She was eighteen. It was her first Season. Surely she had a *few* Seasons. She could flirt with the shelf. Hattie and Anne hadn't made their debuts until twenty, so it seemed only fair that Kitty be allowed to tarry in maidenhood for a while.

These events were just simply too boring.

She would have to start sneaking novels into her bag.

The idea made her smile to herself.

She kept on knitting furiously as a wave of female excitement rippled through the ballroom like wind on a still pond. And she knew exactly why. It was the scandalous Marquess himself.

Lord Curran had arrived.

Late and already foxed, if she was not mistaken.

She shrank yet deeper into the bowl of the egg.

And began to knit with yet more determination.

She refused to look up. She absolutely refused.

But she could feel the energy of it all. And there was an intense amount of it. She gritted her teeth and began to hum to herself. 'Soldiers of Christ, Arise'.

Yes. She was thinking about her Christian duty.

Knit, purl, knit. Purl, knit, purl. Like a soldier marching. The ribbing of the sock would be as fine as any sock in existence, and it would not simply feel like a sop to the bad fortune of having only one foot. It would be a soft and lovely gift. Knit, purl, knit.

She was focusing so intently that she didn't feel the next disturbance in the room around her.

Suddenly there was a clearing of bodies as Lord Boreham made his way through the crowd.

Kitty looked up. She had never spoken to the man before. But he had quite a serious bearing about him.

Not a man she would ever consider as a suitable husband, as he was middle-aged…

Of course, Kitty herself had been accused of behaving in quite a middle-aged fashion more than once. A spinster before her time, it had been suggested—by the Duchess, at least. And Kitty could see the Duchess did not want spinsterhood for her.

If only the Duchess knew how much Kitty aspired to spinsterhood. Though, if she were very honest, widowhood would probably suit her best of all. Perhaps she should be considering an older husband. Widows had ever so much freedom.

She could marry for a brief time, and then find herself free of much societal baggage, conducting herself as she saw fit. All the better if she married a man who already had an heir so she wasn't required to beget them for him.

All of these thoughts went quickly through her head as she watched Lord Boreham look for a target. Truly, the floor was well clear, and he was still looking, craning his head around, as if he could spy no one when he had of course seen her standing there in that rounded space.

She nearly wished to congratulate herself on her clearly perfected art of invisibility. Even *sans corner*, she was very capable of vanishing before the very eyes of a gentleman.

She could see the moment he gave up. Allowed his eyes to settle on her. 'Oh,' he said, as if he had not spotted her before. 'Miss Fitzroy.'

'Lord Boreham,' she said, nodding, not taking her hands off her knitting. Which was perhaps bad form. She supposed she was meant to offer him her hand, but she didn't wish to. And so she didn't.

She was only sorry they'd been formally introduced once before, so that he'd felt he could approach her.

That was one of the other issues she had with London and society at large. There were a great many conventions, and she did not understand them. No matter how the Duchess explained them, with words like, *duty, respectability*, and *propriety*. They meant nothing to her.

It made her wish to ignore them.

Which she sometimes did. People found it shocking. Nearly as shocking as when she brought up conditions in factories, particularly for children. But shouldn't they know that the various goods that they wore, their clothing, was made on the backs of children? Was made at great peril to them. And that wasn't even to get into the sourcing of the material to begin with.

The world was a well of endless horrible unfairness.

And Kitty had yet to figure out exactly what to do about it. She felt small and insignificant, and in truth, the world had been constructed to make her feel that way.

So she did not offer her hand.

It was a rebellion, however small, but an action that she could take.

'These sorts of things are not generally to my liking,' he said.

And what was this? Perhaps he was a kindred spirit. Perhaps she had underestimated him.

The floor had cleared before him, maybe for the same reasons it seemed to clear when Kitty approached others.

'I find them not to my liking either; that's why I am knitting.'

'Yes,' he said. 'You are. Knitting.'

'Yes,' she said, suddenly feeling a spark of vigour. 'I'm knitting a sock for a child who only has one foot. And do you know why he only has one foot?'

'I don't,' he said, his expression suddenly slightly regretful.

'The other was torn off in one of those cotton factories. The machinery is dreadfully unsafe, and children are used because their hands are small, and they can fit their fingers more easily into the mechanisms of the machinery. They are used to climb on it. They also lose hands. Lose fingers. Lose legs…'

'Oh, my,' he said.

'Indeed,' she said. 'And I find it very difficult to forget, particularly when I am surrounded by such fine new fashions made by these very children.'

'I do believe that for the most part fashions are made by a modiste.'

'The fabric,' she said, feeling somewhat impatient.

'Well, it is not often that one finds a young lady given to such conversation. I wonder, though, if you have thoughts on the migration patterns of swallows.'

'I can say with confidence that I do not,' she said.

'It's a fascinating thing,' he returned. 'I have been compiling the scientific journals of…'

And with that, he was off. And it mattered not what she had said about children and their missing limbs, for he was talking about the migration patterns of swallows. In point of fact, Kitty quite liked a bird. And if pressed, she would say that she probably did care about their migration patterns. The rhythm of nature was, after all, an important indicator as to whether or not the world rightly moved in time with the seasons, in time with the patterns of life.

And yet, it seemed in this context to be immaterial. And more to the point he had a way of delivering information in the most righteously boring manner.

Kitty found herself all but melting into the wall, doing her best to keep herself upright. She could see now why everyone had run, and what had she done?

She had marched right into this. She had been certain that she had perhaps found an ally. But no.

There was no ally here.

Only very dull swallows.

'If you will excuse me,' she said, inching away from the wall. 'I've only just seen… It's Lady… I must go.'

She could never be accused of displaying decorous societal behaviours, and she could not be accused of doing so here either. Her need to escape was likely transparent. Yet she made the bid anyway.

Kitty all but scampered across the ballroom looking for a friendly face. Any face.

Most especially looking for Hattie.

Why did Hattie have to go and get married?

Well, she knew why. It was the same reason that Kitty herself needed to find a husband at some point. If not, she would become a dead limb on the family tree, living for ever with the Duke and Duchess of Avondale. Or perhaps she would be able to find employ as a governess? Except she was almost too much a lady for that.

The world was not designed with the freedom of women in mind. In fact, it was very much designed to limit it. Kitty didn't particularly want marriage, it was just a fact that, for a woman of her situation it was undoubtedly the easiest path.

It was only that…Hattie seemed consumed by her new marriage. It was not simply a requirement she had put on, like a new layer of clothing she was forced to wear when going out. She was utterly besotted by her husband.

And Kitty simply couldn't understand.

She found another quiet spot and reached into her bag where she felt her sock, but not the yarn.

Her eyes widened, and she looked across the crowded ballroom, where she saw the yarn unravelling behind her, creating a scarlet red line that trailed in her wake.

She clapped her hand over her mouth and was just beginning to chart her course of action when she saw a masculine hand grab hold of the yarn.

Her heart did something dreadfully uncomfortable as slowly, ever so slowly, the man turned and made eye contact with her from several paces away.

The grin that crossed his face was insouciant, slow and disreputable.

He was the last man on earth she would have wanted collecting her yarn.

Lord Curran had the yarn.

She took a step back, and slowly, ever so slowly, he began to turn the ball as he walked towards her, shrinking the distance between them with each turn, each step. And she froze. Like a small rabbit that had been cornered in her burrow by a fox. Her heart pounded a steady rhythm, and she could feel it at the base of her throat. She despised it. Everything about this. Everything about him.

And as he continued to walk towards her, she itemised the reasons why. Those boots. Butter-soft leather, likely handmade, exquisitely fitted to his calves. A year's wage for a great many people. Those buckskin breeches that seemed to highlight his very flanks, enough to alleviate the poverty in Cheapside for everyone there, for at least a month. Perhaps that was an exaggeration. But perhaps not.

His coat. Black and cut close to his skin like everything else he wore, as if the women around him might miss the fact that he was of the opinion that he cut the finest figure in the ballroom. And there was his face. His face was far too square. Too angular, with a cleft in his chin that seemed excessive. His eyes were startlingly blue, his hair so dark it was nearly black, with just a hint of curl around the edge of his collar.

He did not seem like a real man. Rather he seemed like an artist's rendering.

Draw me the very picture of masculine beauty.

George Claremont. That's who it would be. Too much money, too much arrogance, too much everything.

She found she could not stomach him.

And he *had her yarn*.

He drew closer, and the grin took on a feral glint.

She schooled her mouth into a disapproving frown, and tilted her chin upward.

'Miss Kitty Fitzroy,' he said, her name tripping off his tongue and hitting her with all the impact as if he'd uttered a vile curse. Such was the shock of it.

'You seem to have dropped something.'

She drew up, and tried to look scandalised. As if she cared for formalities and the like. 'I do not believe that we've been formally introduced, sir.'

She had the feeling he did not care.

She had a feeling he revelled in the scandal.

'*Sir.* I quite like the sound of that on your lips. However, do you not think we could dispense with such formalities? You are as aware of who I am, as I am aware of who you are.'

'I beg pardon, but I'm not.'

His smile became incredulous. Good. He deserved incredulity.

He had everything else.

'The Marquess of Curran.'

'Pleasure.' She held out her hand, but not for his, for the yarn ball. But he managed to switch them, and take her gloved hand in his, pinching her fingertips just slightly between his thumb and forefinger. Creating a riot of agony in her soul.

And it *was* agony. For these sorts of events were for the silliest of reasons, and he was the silliest man in attendance at them. And she was being forced to interact with him as if she took it all as seriously as everyone else did.

When, in fact, she knew full well that many people here did not take him seriously in the least; it was simply that they couldn't say anything to the contrary because he was to be a duke someday, and when you were to be a duke someday, it didn't matter what you did in the present. In fact, it didn't matter at all what you did ever, because your title insulated you from the perils of your own behaviour.

She could only imagine what a convenience that was.

She drew her hand away. 'My yarn. Please.'

'What is it that you're making?'

'A noose with which to hang myself. As this evening has grown rather dull.' And off her mouth had gone, racing away without her.

'That seems a bit hysterical, don't you think?'

'I don't know. It depends on how much longer the evening will carry on.'

'Ingenious. To be fashioning your own means of escape, however grim. Though, I do wish to know in truth what you're knitting.'

'Socks,' she said. 'For the children.'

'Oh. *The children.* A worthy cause, no matter who the children are, or where they might be. A worthy cause indeed for a lady of any stripe. The children.'

And it was his mockery that she could not stand. He possessed in his power the ability to ease the woes of many, and yet he mocked her. She might find the Duchess and her efforts to be insufficient, but at least she tried. At least she acted as if she cared a whit for the children. He would mock even the merest scrap of charity when he could not evince any of his own.

'Someone must care for them, do you not think, Lord Curran?' she asked.

'As long as it isn't me.'

'Well no. Why would anyone count on you for such things?'

The corner of his mouth flattened. 'You would speak to me that way?'

'And why not? You spoke to me in similar fashion. You mock me, Lord Curran, as if I am an object of scorn. Or perhaps it is simply that I'm an object beneath your notice. But I see no reason to treat you with deference simply because you have appeared and demanded that I do so with the fit of your boots and breeches. Your title means naught to me. I do not want anything from you. I do not wish to marry you, and I do not need a favour from you.'

'But you do need to marry someone,' he said. 'And do you not think that perhaps my good favour might assist you in finding such a match?'

'If the man in question esteems your opinions, I am not certain I wish to know the gentleman at all.'

'But most people at least pretend to esteem my opinions.'

'And if it is only pretence then it will not impact on the ultimate decision he makes of a wife, do you not think? In fact, if he secretly despises you, he will listen to your report on my character and make note that perhaps I am indeed worthy of his attentions.'

'Yes, perhaps,' he said. And then he dropped the yarn into her upturned palm. 'You had better return to your knitting.' He looked her over with a brutal efficiency that made her feel stripped bare. 'For the children.'

She tilted her chin yet higher. 'I should like nothing more. You had better return to… I am not clear what exactly it is you do.'

He grinned. And the impact of it was as a blow to the stomach. 'Why, Miss Fitzroy, surely you know? My one and only function in this life is to create scandal.'

Chapter Two

What a prickly creature Kitty Fitzroy was. He would be lying if he said he hadn't been intrigued by her from the moment he had first seen her. It was a side effect of the London Season. Boredom. Anyone who did not conform to the clear and obvious pattern set about by society amused him. Not that he could ever betray that. He had no interest in this year's competition for society's most scandalous. This year, he would be taking a wife. Not out of duty to King, country, or title. No. It was for revenge.

Lady Helene Parks would be an excellent choice, daughter of the Marquess of Stanton.

She was suitable for a duchess, though that was not his primary aim.

Her father owned more cotton mills in London than any other single man.

The woman in question did not know that she was the focus of his campaign, but she would soon enough, and when he made his intentions clear, he had no doubt that she would acquiesce.

He was to be a duke after all. And people did react to him with alarming predictability.

Not Kitty Fitzroy.

No. But then, there was nothing predictable about Kitty Fitzroy.

Socks for the children.

It wasn't *socks* the children needed.

He pushed that thought aside, keeping his mask firmly in place. Very few people had any idea he possessed a façade. He had made it a practice to appear as shiny and insubstantial as a mirror. It worked. People saw in him themselves. They forgave his flaws because he exuded what they kept secret.

Consequently, they all feared he could see them.

As if he cared about their base moral failures. Keeping mistresses, indulging in drink to excess, gambling.

He didn't care what sins they played at which harmed their own selves.

It was the carelessness with which they treated the lives of others that made him despise the aristocracy.

And as he was a prominent member thereof, perhaps it wasn't entirely out of line to say that he despised himself.

Dramatic, perhaps, but George did nicely with theatrics. Even in his own mind.

Kitty Fitzroy was not untheatrical herself.

A noose.

He found himself looking over at her again, rubbing the tips of his fingers together as he ruminated on the feel of that soft, crimson yarn she'd been using on the socks.

On the moment when he had taken her hand in his.

She had wanted nothing more than to slap him across the face, he had seen it clearly. And how long had it been since a woman had reacted to him with any sort of vitriol? They never did.

Ever.

Except for her. She did not understand the rules of society, and seemed intent upon flouting them for that very reason.

The poor thing.

She would find out quickly enough that it wasn't the best way to behave.

It wouldn't get her anywhere. It certainly wouldn't get her anything that she wanted.

And that, after all, was the point and purpose to playing any of these games.

You exploited the seriousness with which all of the people around you took these games, and you used them to your ends.

'George.' His friend, Jasper, Earl of Beaufort, approached him and clapped him on the back.

His friends worried for him, he knew. While they knew him well enough to know he wasn't quite as ridiculous as the rest of society believed, they also worried about his excess.

In truth, there was a fair amount of excess. But there was more to it than that. He simply couldn't risk revealing himself. Not even to Jasper and Marcus.

But he didn't mind that.

For all the world, he was feckless George Claremont, rake about town, entirely dependent on his parents' purse strings to support his lavish lifestyle.

Hell, that was even what his father thought of him.

And George merrily spent his father's money, though the man would never know on what.

But he spent too much time with his friends to play the role of debauched playboy entirely straight.

Not that it wasn't a piece of who he was. The work that he did took pieces of his soul.

At least, it had at one time. He felt certain now that he had forfeited the entire thing in these past few years. The tension that he felt, between what he believed was right, and the part he was forced to play was nearly suffocating.

Thankfully his perceived pursuit of the title of 'most scandalous' gave the *ton* something to focus on, and it kept them from ferreting out the real truth about him, which suited him extremely.

'I was just about to take my leave,' George said.

'Really? And where are you off to?'

'My mistress's home. You know I'm keeping a woman in a town house just down the street.'

Jasper's brows shot upward. 'I know no such thing.'

'Do you not? Well, perhaps the news needs to spread.'

Jasper's eyes narrowed. 'What are you up to, George?'

'Congratulations on your nuptials, by the way.'

'You attended them. You've congratulated me already. You've no need to be so dry about it.'

George took a drink of the ratafia in his hand and wished it were something stronger. Stronger would be for later. 'It's just difficult to imagine. You. A married man.'

'Even more difficult to imagine *you* in such a state,' Jasper returned.

'And yet I will be,' he said, scanning the ballroom,

finding the figure of Lady Helene Parks. An assurance. 'By the end of the Season.'

'And what of your mistress?'

He lifted a careless brow. 'What of her?'

'Do you not find that at all at odds with your intent to take a wife?'

'Since when has keeping a mistress been at odds with having a wife?' He adjusted his cuffs. 'I fail to see the moral dilemma you're attempting to knit together here.'

Knitting.

Not a mystery as to why that was at the top of his mind.

'I don't know any more,' Jasper said. 'If this is—'

'I think the mistake that you're making is trying to decipher whether or not there is a *true* me. I am what you see,' he said.

The gulf between himself and his friend widened. But Jasper was a married man now and things were different for him, in a way they never could be for George. Jasper would not approve of his intentions towards Helene Parks. Nor how he intended to conduct himself within that marriage.

Jasper could never know.

'So you want it known you're off to visit a mistress in the middle of the ball?' Jasper said, his tone too knowing.

'I'm definitely not opposed.'

Jasper said nothing, only looked at him with a vague sharpness that George deflected with a smile he hoped looked affected by drink.

He didn't have to hope, he knew how it looked. He was far too practised at this game to fail at it.

'All right then, George,' Jasper said. 'Off with you then.'

George smiled and then went to the entrance of the house where his cloak and hat were given to him. His carriage was at the ready before he stepped foot out into the crisp evening.

The carriage ride down the cobbled lane was quick and loud, the wheels roaring over the uneven surface. 'Wait around back,' he said to his driver as he got out of the carriage.

He straightened his hat and his cloak, and walked up to the door. It was Lily Bell herself who opened it, the former ballerina looking beautiful as always, her blonde hair a-tumble, her body barely contained by her silk robe.

'Lord Curran,' she said, her gaze flicking past him, then over his body. 'You're late.'

'My apologies. Does that mean I'm not welcome?'

'You are always welcome.'

He brushed past her and into the reception area of the town house. His town house. Though it was under an assumed business name so as to keep his affairs private.

George showed his hand freely to all and sundry.

And they never guessed he had an entirely different set of cards hidden beneath the table.

'Shall we get on with it?' he asked.

He couldn't stay long.

He had business to attend. Important business indeed.

Chapter Three

George Claremont's disappearance from the Weatherly ball had created a stir, and had roused an influx of gossip in the scandal rags, which had been passed up and down the rows of town houses in London's finest districts.

'Off with a mistress.' The Duchess clucked at the paper in her hand, and then stopped clucking abruptly when she saw that Kitty was in the room.

'It's salacious,' she said, giving Kitty an apologetic look. 'You want not to be exposed to such things.'

'It is printed in the scandal rags for all to see,' Kitty said. 'I'm hardly being protected from them in any fashion.'

'Indeed not,' said the Duchess, guiltily tucking the scandal rags beneath the corner of her dress. 'How did you find last night's festivities?'

She knew that it would be a poor thing to tell her rather gracious guardian that she hated everything about the London Season. It would be ungrateful. They had given her a debut as if she were one of their own. And she should be astonishingly pleased with that. After the death of her father...

Thinking of that still brought so much pain.

Mourning was a funny thing.

One was prescribed to wear black for a time, and then allowed to wear colour again. As if grief ran along a timeline that you could mark with fashion.

And yet, she had found that that wasn't the reality of death at all.

It wasn't as simple as removing a black shroud. That sadness was an ever-present companion. And she could not find a way to lift it. Her father had been such a thoughtful, generous man, and in many ways, it felt as if the best way to honour his memory was to push forward with her causes.

Obsessively. Relentlessly.

After all, what better way to mark his memory? He would have said that the act of grieving externally like that was pointless. Though he had never taken off his black clothing after the death of her mother.

She did not remember her mother, not overly much.

It had been her father who had had a hand in raising her, who had instilled in her these values. He'd made her care about the world. And then she had been sent out into a world that was even more unfeeling than she had ever imagined, and grappling with all of it, and the brokenness inside her soul over the loss of her father, often felt too big to bear.

On top of all of that, they wanted her to go to parties. They wanted her to find a husband.

It felt a weight too heavy to carry.

'It was lovely,' she said, and she could hear far too well the flatness in her voice.

'You will find a man who excites you,' the Duchess said, grinning. 'And when you do, you will find these events much more to your liking.'

Without permission, her mind cast itself back to her interaction with George. 'The question is whether or not I will find someone at all. I'm too different.'

And that was honest. She did not wish to seem ungrateful, but the truth of it was, she simply wasn't the same as the other ladies making their debuts in society this year. Or any year.

She was from the country, she had never been to London until two years ago, and she had very little concept of these games. Trying to make herself care about it now was nearly impossible. She had wondered on more than one occasion if one simply had to have these things spoken over them from the cradle if they were to find sense in them.

She had not. And so she *could* not.

And yet it was the world she must operate in. The one she must attempt to survive in. She gave not a single care in all the world for the opinion of the *ton*, and yet their opinions could make or break her.

'You will,' the Duchess said, but she could see the older woman falter. Because of course she found Kitty as strange as everyone else did. 'In spite of her accident, Hattie found someone.'

In spite of her accident. The wording of that made Kitty grimace. She could not, however, pretend to misunderstand. Hattie had a perceived handicap due to her injuries. Not dissimilar to the handicap of Kitty's entire personality.

She was not a fool. That was what the Duchess meant. And she did not even mean it unkindly. But it was true all the same.

. The housekeeper came into the room. 'Your Grace,' she said, addressing the Duchess, 'your daughter has arrived for a visit.'

The Duchess stood quickly and smiled. 'Oh, how lovely. Can you get some tea to set out for the three of us?' she asked the housekeeper. She nodded in the affirmative and walked from the room. The Duchess swept after her, clearly far too impatient to wait for Hattie to walk all the way from the hall and into the sitting room.

Kitty took it as an opportunity to seize the scandal sheet. She picked it up and skimmed it with rapt attention.

It was of course largely concerned with the early departure of George Claremont, Marquess of Curran. It was rumoured that he was keeping a mistress in a town house near Covent Garden. Decidedly even more scandalous because surely he was using his father, the Duke's, money to pay for it, as he had no income of his own. In fact, there was a larger rumour that one of the reasons he was rushing to marry—he was rushing to marry? This was news to Kitty—was that he needed to find a wife of means, so that he could continue to live in exactly the debauched way that he wished to live without having to answer to the Duke.

Her opinion of him sank lower. She shook her head,

and when she heard footsteps, she dropped the scandal sheet back into its position on the Duchess's chair and sat primly on the edge of one of the chairs by the sofa. It wasn't that she didn't wish to be caught reading something that the Duchess had deemed inappropriate. It was only that she did not wish to be seen as being interested at all in Lord Curran.

She wasn't interested in him. It was only that he had retrieved her yarn last night and had forced an interaction. Put her in the mind of him, and she did not care for it.

'Kitty!' Hattie greeted her with great excitement, pulling her into her arms and giving her a hug.

It was the sort of exuberance that Kitty wasn't certain she would ever be accustomed to. She appreciated it. She even relished the fact that she had a friend who was so excited to see her, but it was quite a bit beyond her experience of relationships in general.

She patted her cousin's back, returning the gesture as soon as she realised that she had not responded in kind. It was only that this sort of thing still surprised her.

'It's so good to see you,' Kitty said.

'Likewise,' said Hattie.

She wanted to ask her friend so many questions. How was being married? She did not look damaged. Nor did any of her spirit seem dimmed. Quite the opposite, in fact. Though Hattie still walked with a limp—she always would—she seemed renewed in a very particular manner. It wasn't the sort of thing that Kitty associated with marriage.

But then, she did not associate much of anything

with marriage. Except that it felt very like being sold. A transaction, if it was anything.

'We kept missing one another at the ball last night,' Hattie said.

'I didn't even see you,' she said.

'We left quite quickly,' Hattie said, looking regretful. 'Jasper was impatient to get home.'

The Duchess of Avondale gave her daughter a sideways glance, and Hattie schooled her expression into something serene. Kitty did not understand the exchange. But she could understand the desire to leave the ball with haste.

Perhaps another point in the favour of marriage. If she were married, she would not have to attend balls at all...if she married the right sort. There were a great many men who only went to such occasions in order to find a wife. If the man had a wife, then he would not be compelled to go to balls any more. Or at least, not stay the entire evening.

She put a mental tick in the marriage column. It went right along with being provided for, and becoming a widow.

'It is good to see you now,' Kitty said.

She sat back down in the chair, and just then the housekeeper came in with a tray filled with afternoon delicacies. Sandwiches, little cakes, and scones with jam and cream.

She and her father had always taken a rather rustic tea in the afternoon, but she had to admit that tea in London was one thing that outstripped anything she had experienced in the country. She did quite like the food.

She would trade it all, of course, to go back to that life with him. Quiet and lovely.

But no one had offered. So she enjoyed her jam and cream.

'Tell me,' the Duchess said to Hattie, 'all of your particular household gossip.'

And that filled the conversation for quite some time, as Hattie talked about the running of the household, and seemed delighted to do so. Kitty had to wonder if such things were different when it was your own home.

But then, it wasn't truly Hattie's home. It was her husband's. As was Hattie.

And that put a tick in the against marriage column.

'Of course, the most interesting thing is what's been happening at the infirmary.'

And at this Kitty's ears perked up. This was what she had been waiting for. This was why she loved Hattie so dearly. They were kindred spirits in regard to caring for others. It was Hattie who had led her down the path of feeling passionate about child labour, because in the infirmary there were so many children who had been injured in the factories. And they were the lucky ones. By the good graces of somebody they had been brought to the hospital, their bills had been paid for. They had not been left maimed, forced to die in a squalid home of infection.

They had not simply died there in the factory.

And when it wasn't machinery, it was the fires. The mills were tinder boxes, and it was much more common for the workers in those catastrophic fires to perish along with the goods than it should be. They were treated as if they were expendable. Not human.

Hattie cared about injustices like that. It made Kitty feel as though she wasn't quite so alone to have these conversations with her.

'Should you like to go and take a turn about the garden with me?' Hattie asked.

Kitty was grateful for the reprieve from both the sitting room and the Duchess of Avondale.

'Yes. Thank you.'

'Do hurry back,' the Duchess said.

'Don't worry, Mother,' Hattie responded. 'We will return directly.'

Both Kitty and Hattie stood, and Kitty took hold of Hattie's arm, and they walked out of the sitting room and down the back hall, towards the small walled garden behind the town house. 'I did note,' Hattie said, as soon as they were outside, 'that you had quite a long conversation with a certain gentleman at the ball last night.'

She paused for a moment. And her mind was flooded with images of George Claremont.

'If you mean Lord Curran, yes. I could not avoid him. He accosted me after I dropped my ball of yarn.'

Hattie's eyes widened, and she blinked comically. And then she laughed. 'No. I did not mean Lord Curran. I meant Lord Boreham.' She continued to stare at Kitty.

For some reason, Kitty felt ashamed that her first thought had been the Marquess, and not Lord Boreham, with whom she had had quite a long conversation, actually. It was just that when all was said and done, the only person that she'd been able to think of was…

An image filled her mind of him holding her yarn in his outstretched palm.

'Yes. I did speak to him,' she said quickly.

'I did not see you speaking to Lord Curran,' Hattie said.

'It was just before he left. He talked to your husband afterward, then made his abrupt exit, which in fact made the scandal sheets today.'

'You're lucky that *you* didn't make the scandal sheets,' Hattie said. 'Any woman speaking to him is liable to do so.'

'Not me. I would never make the scandal sheets. I am perfectly without scandal. If I had my way, I would have spent the evening tucked into a corner. It was the fact that the room was rather egg-shaped.'

'It was what?'

'It lacked corners. It was shaped like an egg.'

'Oh. Well. I'm sorry for your lack of corners.'

'Thank you,' Kitty said, feeling deeply understood. *Had he understood her best of all?*

'You don't want to give Lord Boredom any ideas, Kitty. You must be more careful about whom you engage in conversation.'

'As I said, I make it my very serious mission to not engage in conversation at such events.'

Hattie looked at her, her expression growing tender. 'But you must find yourself a husband,' she said. 'It is the way of things.'

'You have found it… What I mean to say is, you are not abused?'

'Of course not. Jasper is wonderful. He is nothing like what people think. All that scandal. He has a very good heart.'

'But you live with him. And you…you are facing the prospect of having his heirs.'

'You make it sound as if I'm facing the guillotine.'

'In my mind it is not too dissimilar to the guillotine.'

'You will find a man that you have something in common with. That you enjoy making conversation with. The choice is yours. No one is going to force you into marriage with somebody that you don't wish to be with.'

'You're not suggesting that I'm going to fall in love.'

She looked sad. 'I would very much like for you to fall in love. I have.'

'We must acknowledge that it is extremely unlikely.'

'I don't have to do any such thing, Kitty,' Hattie said.

But Kitty could see that Hattie did think it was quite a far-fetched idea. And Kitty was all right with that. She did not have fantasies of falling in love. She did not think much of romance. Perhaps because she was too practical.

'I would be happy with mutual understanding,' Kitty said. 'And perhaps someone who will leave me a widow directly.'

Hattie laughed. 'You must not make that part of your introductory conversation with the man you hope to marry.'

'Of course not. I know better than that.' Except, she might. She made a note in her mind.

'Tomorrow you have yet another party, are you feeling up for it?'

'No. But then, I never am. I do have it on good authority that there will at least be corners in this ballroom.'

'There ought to be.'

'Well. There are always things to be thankful for.'

Hattie, and corners. And in the moment, she was thankful for both. Very deeply.

Chapter Four

It was difficult to avoid sinking into the depths of despair when the reward for finishing one party was to have to wake up the next day and begin preparations for another one.

Kitty felt immensely long-suffering, even with her cousin Annie's cheerful company. It was strange, it just being the two of them in the house. Without Hattie, who was married and off on her own.

'What do you think Hattie is doing right now?' Annie asked. Their maids giggled, and Annie and Kitty exchanged a glance. They didn't know what was so funny.

'I don't know,' Kitty said. 'But I'm not sure that I can say I look forward to meeting the same fate.'

'Not even if the man is very handsome?'

'I'm not certain what aesthetics have to do with it. It is…a limiting of freedom.'

'I'm not certain about that,' Annie said, her brow wrinkling critically. 'It seems as if it is a trading of freedoms.'

Perhaps Annie was right about that. There were certain things a young, unmarried lady could never do, that a married woman could.

She thought back to the strict talking to she'd been given by the governess when she had first arrived at the Duke and Duchess of Avondale's. She had been taught all of the things that a woman ought to do and ought not to do. The list for unmarried ladies was unspeakably long and the rules didn't make sense to her. Sometimes she found herself on the wrong side of them.

The intensity of it had made Kitty feel as though she was being crushed. Truthfully, most of the things that had been mentioned were activities that Kitty herself had never engaged in in any way—she had certainly never been alone with a gentleman. But it was the presence of that which she ought not to do, the sheer volume of such things, that made her feel as if she was suffocating.

'What sort of man do you suppose you will marry?'

Kitty frowned. 'I don't know. I should like to have a couple of Seasons to think about it. This is only my debut, and I am hardly the sensation of the *ton*.'

That was putting it quite mildly.

'I think people are fascinated by you,' Annie said. But of course, her cousin would give her such a vote of confidence. She was far too sweet to say otherwise.

'I think that people are only fascinated by me in terms of what might come out of my mouth next. I did spend fifteen minutes lecturing a host on the ways in which sugarcane is produced and brought to England.'

'Yes,' Annie said. 'You did. But there is great value

in such an education, and people should not be so thoughtless.'

'I have always thought so,' Kitty said, examining herself yet more closely in the mirror.

She did not often give a thought to her looks. They did not matter. She had dark hair, and she had always found that her features reminded her slightly of a field mouse—such as her upturned nose, with freckles sprinkled across it.

'I should like a man who is not vain,' Kitty said. She thought of George Claremont. He would not qualify. He was vanity personified, and he would, of course, choose a woman who was stunningly beautiful, to match his own startlingly good looks.

But of course, that would require that he married. And though it was rumoured that he was set on marrying, he did not behave like a man who was courting anyone in particular.

'That is a good quality, I think. Not possessing vanity,' Annie said seriously.

'And that should go for the way he views me. I should like for him to see me as something more than a jewel to be added to a collection, do you not think?'

Annie nodded gravely. 'Yes. I would think.'

'And I should not like to be forced into anything. Look at what happened to poor Freddie and Dorothea.'

Annie went quiet. 'Oh, yes. Freddie ought to be ashamed of himself.'

'Ought he to?'

Freddie Fitzroy, Hattie and Annie's older brother, was, of course, a rather scandalous figure, being that he was a Fitzroy, after all. In fact, if anyone were to rival George Claremont for rakish behaviour, it would be her cousin Freddie, who had been named society's most scandalous last year when he had eloped with George's sister Dorothea Claremont. Their whirlwind love affair had left Kitty with more questions than answers.

She could not remember her own parents. Not together. It was a tragedy, she thought, that she had been robbed of seeing real love such as that up close.

Her father had upended his entire life for their mother. She had not been a lady but the parlour maid. It had created such a scandal at the time. They had moved away from London, away from society, to the country, where they could simply be, and not be hounded by scandal.

And scandal sheets. It was one reason that Kitty found all of it so appalling. She knew how it had tried and tested her parents. How hard they had fought for their love.

She could not imagine loving in such a way. She could not imagine wanting to. She felt consumed instead by causes, by concerns. She did not worry about her own comfort. Her own needs. Not when there were so many other needs gone unmet in the world.

'I shouldn't like to be caught up in a scandalous marriage. With the way the Claremonts and Fitzroys have always hated each other, that Freddie is now saddled with them as family...' Annie said.

Indeed. Kitty could think of nothing worse.

Her parents had endured scandal and speculation for

love. Kitty herself was willing to do it to effect change. Those seemed the only two worthy reasons for scandal.

And even then, Kitty did not have great aspirations towards love.

In fact…she didn't wish to feel it.

Her mother's death had nearly destroyed her father. Her memories of being a small girl were that Papa had never smiled.

It had taken him ages to get that smile back. And then he had died. But at least Kitty had had him in her childhood. Still, it was not the greatest testament to love.

Losing him had been like losing a limb. She should not like to ever experience something like that again.

'What of you, Annie? What sort of husband would you like?'

'Hattie seems so happy with the Earl of Beaufort. And they seem to…share such great affection for one another. Have you noticed the way he is always touching her hand? The way he touches her back when she walks into a room?'

Kitty had noticed that. She tried to imagine being so familiar with a man that he might put his hands on her in that way.

And for some reason, her mind could only conjure up images of George Claremont. She banished the thought altogether. He was the last man on earth she would ever want to find herself in an assignation with. And yet, she could not forget the way he had touched her yarn.

His hands were large, and he had made the bright red spool of yarn look so small.

No. She was fascinated by him simply because he was as different from her as it was possible for her to be from another human being.

He was…he was a force, and therefore difficult to ignore. Large and angular and loud. He charmed groups of people. At every ball there was an entire circle of acolytes surrounding him, laughing uproariously like a flock of crows. She found it distasteful. The way men and women hung upon his every word as if his take on fashion, gossip or wicked takedowns of those around them were the height of wit.

Granted, based on bits she'd observed here and there, he did have wit. But his wit was sharp, a rapier. Mean if it was anything.

She did not know why anyone countenanced him.

'I think I should like that,' Annie said. 'That care.'

'I should like someone who cares about the same things that I do. A friend. I think that is the part of Hattie's marriage that I admire so much. They seem to always have something to say to one another. It is why we barely see her even at a ball. It is desperately unfashionable to be so enamoured of one's husband.' As if Kitty cared about fashion. It was merely an observation.

'Indeed,' Annie said. 'I think I should like to be unfashionably taken with my husband.'

'I think I should like him to be unfashionably outspoken. In the same way that I am. That way, we will either change the way of the world, or people will cease inviting us to parties altogether.'

Annie smiled. 'Not a terrible thought.'

And Kitty added that to the column in her mind that

was decidedly for finding a husband. If she found one as off-putting as herself, they could avoid balls.

As she looked at herself, made up expertly for this particular party, and wearing a pale blue gown that rather put parts of her body on display she wished to cover, she thought that might be the best reason of all.

Chapter Five

George was exhausted. He was accustomed to burning the candle at both ends. It was required. He had to be able to show up at these sorts of parties and put on the face that was expected of him, and he had work to do.

The truth was, the more disreputable he looked when he arrived at these events, the later he was, and the more exhausted, the better. Because it suggested a late night of debauchery. If only they knew.

But they never could.

The work George did was accomplished because of the secrecy. If his true thoughts were ever known he would lose access to the rooms where it all happened.

He could not afford that.

Ever.

He was on the verge of committing to this façade for life.

He would do nothing to disrupt that.

He looked across the broad expanse of the room, and saw Lady Helene Parks. Tonight, he would make it his goal to cement his connection with her. And at the house party a fortnight from now, he would make his intentions plain. He would secure permission from her father the morning he arrived and make his proposition to her that same night.

He had it all planned, and nothing would divert him from course now.

Except Lady Abernathy separated herself from the crowd of people she was standing in, and began to walk towards him, her gaze intent, her bosom spilling over the neckline of her gown. He knew what she wanted. And she thought of course it was for her to have, because she had made her way through the beds of the various gentlemen in the *ton* with astonishing vigour in the years since her husband passed, and rumour would have it that George had a bed that was open to all and sundry. So of course she would feel she made this particular grade.

He did not have time to toy with her, though there had been a time when he might have.

A particular crawling sensation moved over his skin. That was the thing he hated most. The George Claremont mask was not half so much a mask as he might've liked. He was capable of the sorts of bloodless couplings that society believed he engaged in on a regular basis. More than capable of it.

Shallow, soulless evenings spent satisfying the lust of the flesh and nothing more. Women whose names and faces he could not recall, a blur of the sort of pleasure that left the pit in one's stomach once it was satisfied. Sometimes he found his disdain of the people around him particularly hypocritical, considering that in practice, he was truly one of them.

He could not disdain Lady Abernathy, even if he did not wish to spend the evening with her.

He could not disdain her, because he was her.

It was just he had a different goal now than satisfying his baser needs.

'George,' she said, not bothering with a title, her expression coquettish. 'I do hope that you're not planning on leaving early tonight as you did the other night.'

'If you know that I left early, then you know why,' he said, keeping his gaze icy as he allowed it to move over her curves. He felt nothing as he examined her admittedly fine form. One female body, lovely though it might be, was the same as the next. It did not matter whom he took to his bed.

It never had.

'Yes,' she said. 'Rumour has it you have a rather serious mistress that you're keeping in style.'

'Indeed.'

'I don't see why that has to be an impediment to us enjoying an evening.'

Good God, she was direct. At another time, he might've appreciated that. He did not like dealing in word games.

'Not at this moment,' he said. 'I find that I'm otherwise engaged tonight.'

'I feel a gentleman can always change his mind.'

'Perhaps. But I am not a gentleman. Not in deed, in any case.' He departed, and began to move yet more quickly through the crowd, but she followed and as she put her hand on his back, he reached out and grabbed the hand of the nearest young lady. 'I have promised a dance to—' He looked and saw that he had taken hold of Kitty Fitzroy. Why was this woman suddenly everywhere?

She was looking at him as if he had dropped a living slug into her palm, rather than his gloved hand.

'Yes. Miss Fitzroy,' he said to Lady Abernathy. 'I have filled a space in her dance card, and I must honour that stolen spot.'

And with that, he swept her towards the dance floor, away from Lady Abernathy.

'What are you doing?' she asked, looking wildly about the room.

'Do endeavour to stop looking as though I am dragging you to your knitted noose,' he said. 'I'm taking you to the dance floor.'

'I didn't even *bring* a dance card,' she said. 'I've nothing to fill.'

'Oh, good. Then I have not impinged upon another man's territory.'

She frowned, her delicate brows swooping downwards. 'Do not mock me.'

'I'm not mocking you.'

'You are. You know that there is no other man that has asked me to dance tonight. Nor any night. I have never gone out to the dance floor.'

He took her other hand and pulled her near him in a closed position. 'Until now.'

It was a waltz, and that brought her small, perfect form only an inch or so away from his body. He preferred a waltz for that reason. If he was going to dance, he liked to have the woman pressed against him.

Of course, he had not thought he would end up holding Kitty Fitzroy.

She looked up at him, her blue eyes wide and dewy with panic.

'Kitty,' he said, his tone more stern than intended. 'Breathe.'

She obeyed, and her breasts rose. Slight though they were, his eye was drawn to them. He was a man, after all.

If he were fully in character, he might pull her more firmly against him so he could feel the nuances of those curves against his chest.

He wondered what the hell the girl would make of such a thing. She was so serious. Always frowning, at least at him. She seemed far too innocent to have ever had such a thought enter her mind.

All the more reason to stay away from her.

Yet here she was in his path again.

She looked around and he wanted to take hold of her chin and steady her. 'I feel foolish,' she said.

He did not take hold of her chin. 'Feel free to scamper off the dance floor.'

'I would feel yet more foolish,' she said, as they whirled around the dance floor.

'I would hate to compound your foolishness.'

She looked around, her eyes wide. 'People are staring.'

'Of course they are. I'm the Marquess of Curran. I'm very interesting.'

She tilted her head to the side and he saw it. The fire there. She couldn't resist. She loved to strike at him. The dear little snake. 'Do you think so? Because I think you're rather predictable.'

'Oh, dear,' he said, in mock horror. 'What a disappointment.'

'I don't think you're disappointed.' A touch of colour rose in her cheeks.

He found he enjoyed sparring with her. People were so… Typically they were incredibly obsequious, and he found it boring.

They wrote about him in the scandal sheets, and there they would say what they really thought. That he was shocking. That he was a disgrace. Spending his father's money on outlandish and disgraceful affairs.

He found it refreshing, if nothing else. They might be wrong, but at least it was honest. None of this falling all over themselves to curry his favour to his face while whispering about him behind their hands.

Kitty, of course, did not whisper. She did not try to gain favour. In fact, she'd told him she did not wish a favour from him ever. Though he might now owe her one.

He looked over her shoulder and he could see three of the biggest scandalmongers in the *ton*—Lady Peregrine, Lady Balfour and Dame Bainbridge. He suspected they were the authors of the most popular scandal sheet in London, though it could not be proven. Currently, they had all eyes on himself and Kitty.

That amused him.

What would they make of that? He was the scandal

of the century, let alone the Season, and Kitty was a wallflower.

He looked down at her and was stopped by the curve of her neck. It was an extremely elegant curve, and haughty.

That, he realised just then, was one thing he found so fascinating about Kitty Fitzroy.

She seemed shy, hiding in corners and knitting, but he did not think she was shy. She had a deeply ingrained sense of herself. Her opinions were always right there, at the surface of her, as was her every emotion.

If he was a mirror, Kitty was a window. To look at her was to see inside.

It did not speak to the sort of timidity one usually ascribed a wallflower.

Very suddenly, he laughed. And as he did her breath caught and hitched her chest up, the tips of her breasts brushing against him. He felt it.

'What?' she asked.

He chose to believe she was asking about the laugh, not his notice of her breasts touching him. 'It occurred to me just now, that you do not like us, do you, Miss Fitzroy?'

She wrinkled her nose. 'Us?'

'Society.'

'I do not dislike every person here,' she said. 'But I find myself perplexed and baffled by the structure itself.'

'You find yourself above us, don't you? It is why you stand in corners. Not because you fear us, because you believe yourself to be better.'

She shook her head, her dark hair catching the candle-light, revealing a rich gold and warm mahogany he had not before noticed. This girl was filled with surprises. She should not be, transparent as she was.

The issue was not that she hid, it was that no one had looked.

'I do not think myself better, but I do think I will only end up giving a lecture on the state of the world, the need at the infirmary, the unnecessary excess of the *ton*…'

'Well that would not be popular.'

'Indeed not. My aunt and uncle—that is, the Duke and Duchess of Avondale—they have been very kind to me. I am not trying to make all of their friends hate me. Only, my chest burns with conviction, and I fear if I do not speak it will consume me and so…it is better to stand in the corner and knit.'

She spoke freely then, not in icy barbs trying to score points on him. And he saw then, the passion in her. The fire.

She was not a wallflower. She was more a Valkyrie. Standing, waiting. And once it was time, she would unleash fury.

'Tell me, Kitty, what will you do with all that fire when it burns out of control? Because it will. Because you will burn, and all that passion in you will consume you, and what then?'

His voice came out harder than he intended. Rougher.

He had total control over himself at all times; he had to, playing games such as he did.

But he looked at her and he *saw* her.

He knew what she felt. That burn of injustice.

'I…'

She had no words then, a rarity. She seemed caught. And he realised then she was staring. At his eyes and then…at his mouth.

He spun her, and pulled her against him, and her eyes went wider, her lips parting slightly. He felt the impact of her, the soft weight of her.

He had no call to linger on it.

The music ended, and they stood a moment. His breathing was laboured. Certainly not from the exertion of a mere waltz. And Kitty beat a hasty path away from him. She tucked herself away in a far, dimly lit corner.

He could not see her. Not to his satisfaction.

He wondered if she was knitting. And decided it was of no consequence. Because what he needed to do was make his way to Helene. He had already been delayed long enough.

And there she was, looking wholesome and lovely. His eyes moved easily over her. She had plump curves and a round face. She was *easy* to look at.

Kitty felt sharp.

He moved through the crowd until he came to where Helene was standing, a bit of a knowing smile on her face. It made him wonder if she was an innocent at all. He didn't mind. In fact, given his ulterior motive, he would like it if she had some secrets of her own. It would make her feel like fairer quarry.

Poor little Kitty…there was nothing knowing in her smile.

You haven't seen her smile.

'Good evening, Lady Helene,' he said.

'Good evening, Lord Curran,' she said. 'I had thought that you might not find your way to me.'

'I will always find my way to you,' he said.

He heard a faint choking sound and looked and saw that Kitty Fitzroy was well within earshot, and seemed to have taken offence at what he'd said.

His eyes met hers. He wished to go shake the little wretch by her shoulders. She should not be eavesdropping.

He looked back at Helene. 'I trust you've had a pleasant evening thus far.'

'It has only got more pleasant.'

He heard the sound again. 'Dreadful,' he said, making a tutting sound. 'Seems as if someone has taken ill and should perhaps have stayed home this evening.'

'Oh, dear,' Helene said, her eyes round. 'I'm afraid of taking ill. I do not wish to be bled with leeches.'

'Better to be bled with leeches than with badgers, if pressed. One has proven to be vastly worse for your health.'

'What?' Helene blinked.

He heard yet another small sound from Kitty's corner, and he reared around to look at her. She was laughing.

And there it was, a smile.

A mean little smile.

He found he wanted... Well, what it did was... It was as if there was a match that had been struck on the column of his throat, trailing heat and fire in its wake.

He looked away from Kitty. 'We ought to dance,' he said.

Anything to get him out of the proximity of that little pest. And that was how he found himself out on the dance floor with Lady Helene.

He would consign the interaction with Kitty to the recesses of his memory. She was inconsequential. The fact that she seemed perennially near meant nothing.

None of this meant anything.

He looked at the beautiful, insubstantial woman he held in his arms.

No. None of this really meant anything at all.

Chapter Six

Kitty was in a fury. An absolute fury. How dare he dance with her in front of all these people? How dare he…how dare he touch her as he had done? She hadn't wanted him to do that. She did not care for him, not in the least. And he had… It was a joke. And everyone knew it. Everybody knew that he was not the sort of man who would ever dance with her, not under other circumstances. Not under any sort of normal circumstances. It was so apparently clear that he had been using her.

And she did not care. Not really. Not when in the grand scheme of things there were so many other atrocities that her own pride did not signify.

And yet, she found it wounded her.

She had not thought she had any sort of feminine ego to her credit.

But perhaps it was the absurdity of it. She was not a great beauty. She was a rather drab…well, sparrow, perhaps. Though she wondered if Lord Boredom would've called her shallow. And then she decided it didn't matter. Not truly. All she knew was that she would never be called a suitable match for George Claremont.

Quite apart from the fact that their families had a rift that went back decades. Though, she knew very little about it. Her own father had been so separate from London, and the politics therein, even concerning his own family. He had fallen in love, and he had gone away from it all. Her mother had not been a society type, and her father had moved heaven and earth to make her happy.

She would never be loved like that. It was such a rarity, that sort of connection. She did not feel sorry for herself. It was simply true. And it was all right. But she did want something other than the sort of mercenary arrangement she saw happening around her. She just wasn't certain if that were possible considering that, in her estimation, the entire concept of marriage with someone was inherently mercenary.

But she knew that there were marriages that were happy. She had not had the opportunity to see as much of her mother and father's relationship as she might like. But she had known there was real love between them because her father had changed his entire life to better suit his wife. And that, as far as Kitty was aware, was love.

She felt restless, flushed with shame, and immensely, irrationally perturbed by the fact that George was now dancing with Lady Helene Parks. She was inestimably more beautiful than Kitty. She did not… It was not that she felt a particular… It was simply what it was. And everyone had witnessed George leave her for Helene.

She felt in that moment exceedingly silly to be concerned about such a thing.

And yet she was.

And then, much to her great relief, Hattie seemed to materialise from nothing and join her in the corner.

'Are you quite well?'

'As a matter of fact, I am not.'

'What has happened?'

'I do not wish to dance with Lord Curran.'

'I should not have thought so,' she said. 'You have made your distaste for him quite apparent to me.'

'He took me off guard.'

'Of course he did.'

'And now he is dancing with her. As if to make contrast between the two of us.'

'Is that what you think, Kitty?'

'I don't know. It is said that these sorts of mating rituals that humans involve themselves in mirror the rituals that animals engage in as well. And they are ruthless and insensible sorts of things.'

'You speak of mating, Kitty?' she said, questioning her intently. And Kitty suddenly felt prickly warm.

'That is not what I mean. Except...' Her mind was quite fuzzy on the details of such things. She only knew that she was supposed to be embarrassed about it. And so effective was that projected embarrassment, she actually found that she was. Unlike other arbitrary societal dictates, this one made her feel quite on edge.

'What I mean is it is a ritual. A game. That's what it is. A game. A game that we play in ballrooms, and yet it determines the course of the entirety of the young woman's life.'

'A man's too,' Hattie said.

'No,' Kitty protested. 'Not a man's. A man does what he will, before and after marriage. The game of scandal for men is simply that. A game. It is not a game for women, is it? If we do not marry what will become of us? If we are subject to a scandal severe enough, what will become of us?'

'Kitty, you do not have to be concerned about the soul of the entire world every single day for the whole of the day.'

'But I can't help it,' she said.

'Sometimes a party is simply a party. And a dance is simply a dance. I do not think he sought to make fun of you.'

'I do. There is nothing about George Claremont that suggests he is anything other than a reprobate.'

Hattie patted her hand. 'You should knit. It does soothe you.'

'I should,' she agreed.

She should do anything other than leer at George as if...

Why was she thinking of him by his given name? It was preposterous.

She looked at the way he moved with Helene. She was quite the most beautiful thing. And she looked at him as if he had set the stars in their place. He probably loved that. Couldn't get enough. He was the sort of man who would take worship as his due. He grinned at her, and there was something about what a smile did to his face.

Kitty could not help but notice, though, that the smile never seemed to reach those blue eyes of his.

They were beautiful eyes. But they did not contain the joy of a fool. That stopped her short. For she had noticed that people she often thought of as foolish had a feckless sort of happiness about them. As if they were unconcerned and untouched by all the evils in the world. It was not that she thought happiness in and of itself was a foolish thing. There was just a type of happiness that she associated with those who cared for nothing but themselves.

It was not there in George Claremont, the Marquess of Curran's, eyes. And it was a strange realisation.

She looked back at Hattie. 'It is of no consequence. He is of no consequence to me. This is my debut Season. I suppose I am to be about the business of finding a husband.'

'You don't want one?'

She shook her head. 'No. That does not matter, though, does it?'

'No. I'm sorry, Kitty. It doesn't.'

'There are far too many things in this world to fight. This being one of them. But I do not suppose that I can fight everything else that I wish to do battle against while also fighting for my own survival.'

'That is indeed true.'

'And so, I must take care to secure myself a match.'

'Likely.'

'Even the lord of scandal must do that,' she said.

'I guess none of us is free of it.'

'Not truly.'

That, at least, felt like a small spot of justice. And so she clung to that. Because there really was little else.

Chapter Seven

And so the Season went on much in that same fashion that it had begun. With scandal and breathless stories written about it. Kitty began to recognise that the ballroom was not dissimilar to a battlefield. Her position in the corner was her ready position. From it she could fend off those advancing, and no one could come at her from behind. She found ways to retreat if need be.

And she also had a primary foe.

George Claremont, the Marquess of Curran, was ever in her path. No matter what.

He was always and ever the subject of the scandal sheets. Leaving the ball to associate—supposedly—with his ballerina mistress, and at the same time courting Helene Parks. The *ton* was alight with the gossip that he would soon be proposing to the young heiress. She was wealthy, and of course her purse would keep him in the lifestyle to which he had become accustomed. The dowry that she would come with would set them up handsomely, and he would no longer have to seek his father's approval for his excesses. Of course, everyone shook their heads sadly of the fate that awaited Helene. She would be a lonely woman, destined to spend evenings at her house all alone while her husband paraded about town, brothels and other various dens of iniquity—his true home—while the hearth in the manor would burn, waiting for him to arrive. Yet he never would.

The fascination with him truly turned Kitty's stomach. He was not fascinating. He was an arse of the highest order.

And she did not even feel the slightest bit guilty thinking of him as such. Not that she would say it aloud.

Another tactical manoeuvre was steering clear of Lord Boredom.

He had found in Kitty a listening ear. At least, he seemed to think so. Which meant that Kitty had to run twice as fast when she saw him arrive.

The last thing she wanted was to get trapped in another monologue about swallows. Or worse yet, snails. There had been an entire conversation based around garden snails, and truly, Kitty was quite the person to speak of such odd topics with, but he managed to make all of it exceedingly dull, and in the back of her mind was always the screeching terror that he might be thinking of her as potential material for a wife. She could not bear it. There were any number of older men that she could perhaps consign herself to a short lifetime with. But he was not one of them. She would never be able to manage it. She would never be able to make it. It was beyond the pale. It could not be borne.

The trouble with this particular party was that it was a dinner party. And that brought with it an entirely new set of issues, issues that Kitty didn't particularly want to deal with. But then, since when did she ever want to deal with the issues inherent in engaging in society?

She didn't. But no one asked. And, even if they did, it would only be with the faint politeness of the *ton*. None of it would be real. And none of it would mean anything. The issue at dinner parties was there was no quarter to hide in. It was inevitable that you would be seated next to someone, and with people across from you as well. It was a veritable social box. One that she had yet to figure out how to escape.

When she entered this particular dining room, the Duke and Duchess of Avondale were with her, and she hoped that she might find herself sitting near them. But instead, they put the debutantes down at their own end of the grand table. And what a table it was. Set with fowl—pheasant and quail—along with fish and eels, which Kitty could not say she was a particular fan of. But again, no one had asked her. She was seated, and the chair to her left remained empty. She hoped that it would stay thus.

On her right, was Lord Boredom.

It seemed that Kitty had been put at the very edge of the debutantes. Or maybe, someone was having a laugh at her expense. Lord Boredom, after all, was single. Maybe they had decided that Kitty would be a good potential match for him.

'It is very good to see you again, Miss Fitzroy,' he said.

And for the first time ever, Kitty found she hoped

that the seat next to her would end up being filled, and soon. Directly across from her was Lady Penelope Celevenger, another young debutante in her first Season, though Kitty did not know her well. Next to her was the rather dashing Earl of Wainscott. The two of them seemed to have a rapport, and Kitty supposed that's why they were seated next to one another. Which made her even more suspicious of Lord Boredom being placed to her right.

'And you see, Miss Fitzroy,' Lord Boredom was saying, 'I have been ill for some days. And I find it really does drain me of my figure to be stricken so with lurgy. It is an astonishing thing to me, the way that females carry on with their duties when stricken with similar. Men have hardier constitutions, of course. It is well known. However, I do wonder if it is a very trick of the devil that such illnesses affect men that much more profoundly.'

Kitty blinked, biting her lip to keep from saying: perhaps it is simply that men have responsibilities which might be more easily shoved aside.

At least, men of his station.

Perhaps it was simply that they could be so confident in the fact that the women in their lives would care for them. Whereas women often had no such assurance. Though she imagined if they had a full staff they might.

'I still feel a bit weak.' And then he sniffed. It was a great, wet sort of sound, and it made Kitty wish she were dead, and that she did not have an eel on her plate.

She looked down the table at the scandal sheet ladies. They were watching them. The two of them.

No. She could not face such a fate. Could not face such a fate as to be written up with Lord Boredom in the scandal sheets.

She cursed whoever was supposed to be sitting on her left. She cursed them to the devil. Because she would happily make conversation with them, while she could not gain the attention of the Earl of Wainscott or Lady Penelope, because they were both so entranced with one another. Why didn't the scandal writers write about them? Because they were probable? Because there was nothing to mock? It was truly unfair. All of this.

'That reminds me of some of the very fascinating medical research I've been reading about. I'm not certain if you will have the interest or capability of comprehending, given that you are quite young, and female, but I should like to try to explain it to you all the same.'

'Miss Fitzroy' came a sharp voice from down the other end of the table. And she realised it was one of the scandal sheet writers. 'I noted that you were knitting a few occasions ago. Rather than dancing. Though, we did note that you danced at the previous event.'

Of course they had noted her dance with Lord Curran. Yet for some reason, they were asking about her knitting. She did not think it was to be kind. But she also saw little point in answering in any way other than honestly.

'Yes. I do often knit.'

'And what were you making? I heard that it was a very small sock. One is tempted to think that there is perhaps a blessed event coming for someone in the *ton*. Only I have not heard a thing.'

She was looking for gossip? Probably about Hattie. And she couldn't have it any more wrong. 'No. The socks are not for the child of anyone I know. The socks are for children at the infirmary. There are many children there recovering from serious illness and injury.'

'Oh, dear,' the woman said. 'Surely there cannot be quite so many children taken with injury. Certainly not any I've heard of.'

'Because they're not children anyone here concerns themselves with. Not in any way other than the occasional gifting of a basket of food. A bandage for what is a mortal wound.'

She could feel that fire rising in her breast. Could feel the eyes at the table beginning to linger on her. Could feel other conversations slow and then stop altogether. But she could not stop herself. She could not.

'Do tell?' the woman said. She looked like a praying mantis. All angular and ready to strike. She did not mean well, and Kitty knew it, and yet she simply did not possess the skill of being…of being not who she was. Of being not what she was. She did not possess the ability to be dishonest. And she had a moment to speak of what mattered, and if even one person at the table was affected by her speech, how could she not take the moment? These were all the people who had the power to do something.

Kitty herself had no power at all. She had nothing other than the burning desire to make change. She could not fix this. She could not fix anything. Unless she spoke. Knitting wasn't enough. She was here for a reason. She hadn't chosen to be.

Maybe this made it matter. Moving to London. Losing her father. If she worked hard enough at this, maybe it could all matter.

'There is an epidemic of child labour occurring in London. How do you think you come about your fine clothes at such reasonable prices?'

'Factories,' one of the men said. 'It has made goods much cheaper.'

'Yes. But most especially the cost can remain low if those employed are paid nearly nothing. And many of those employees are children. The environment is dangerous. And they are easily wounded. Sometimes killed. There are also unknown issues created by days spent in an environment where so much debris is floating through the air. In the north of the country, there are stories of children who cough like men who have spent years in coal mines. It is happening here too. And that is when they are not mortally wounded or killed in fires or accidents with machinery. And so I knit socks. Because I am not in Parliament, and I do not possess the power to make laws that require children to be given a safe work environment, or to be allowed to be children, and to not be working at all.'

'It is what the poor do,' a woman said. 'They work. If they do not, they do not eat.'

'And yet you've never worked a day in your life, and look at you sitting here with plates of food on the table. You inherited it. You were lucky. Born into your position by good chance of genetics. And so they must work, while you disdain it? Children must?'

'Please,' said the host. 'Miss Fitzroy. We are trying to enjoy a meal.'

She looked down the table at the Duke and Duchess of Avondale, who had expressions akin to horror on their faces. They were taking care of her, and she had embarrassed them.

Embarrassment isn't fatal. But working in those factories can be.

She appreciated her own internal monologue attempting to justify this behaviour to herself. But the fact was, she had spoken out of turn and now she felt as if she was going to cry. Every eye at the table was turned to her. And she wished for a second that she could turn it all back, and simply listen to Lord Boredom talk about his medical research while she tried to eat an eel, because it would be infinitely preferable to this moment of fiery defiance that was now mingled so intensely with shame.

'If you'll excuse me,' she said. 'I must freshen my toilette. I shall be but a moment.'

She got up from the table, and all but fled the room. Nearly running down the hall, not caring if she found it necessary or not. It didn't matter. She just needed a moment. A moment to not feel quite so…as though she was related to the fish on the table. Out in the open air where she did not belong, gasping.

She needed to be back in the country. She needed solace.

And that was when she saw the doors open to a terrace outside. And no one was on it. Everyone was of course sitting at the dinner table.

She gathered herself and went outside. Wrapping her hands over the top of the balustrade she looked out into the darkness. She let her eyes close, let the breeze move across her face. The way this home was situated at the edge of the city allowed for more expansive gardens. Allowed for Kitty to imagine for a moment that she might be back where she belonged. That she might be back in the country.

'Oh, Papa,' she whispered. 'You would be sorry that I was here, right back in the world you left. Subject to the same rules you ran from. You would not like this. And yet I can hardly turn away from it, can I? How can I? I wish that I could. But I have to make my own way, and I know that you loved me, but you did not leave me much in the way of financial means. I am property. And in order to live I must remain property.' She let the breeze wash over her. And it was then that she smelled smoke. From a cheroot.

She opened her eyes, and looked to her left, and down the other end of the terrace, draped over the balustrade, was a male figure. She could see the glowing red end of the cheroot, and very little else. The figure was tall.

And suddenly, she knew who it was. Because she felt it. That same feeling she always did when she saw him. A sort of violent explosion at her midsection that spoke of…it had to be her dislike of him. Because what else could it be? And yet, he was like something inevitable. Undeniable. He was always there. Even when he wasn't. His was the empty chair. Of that she was certain.

She thought back to the other night when he had

picked up her yarn and brought it to her. Whoever had arranged the seating tonight must surely have been watching the proceedings of the night in the egg-shaped ballroom. Because her seating chart involved both Lord Boredom, and George Claremont. Of course, Lord Curran had not bothered to sit down at the table. Why would he be where he was expected? Why would he be where she wanted him to be, the one time she wanted him there? Instead he was out here. Where she did not wish him.

She wondered if he had seen her. Of course he had. *You're out here talking to yourself.*

She wondered if he knew who she was.

And then, the red glow straightened. 'Miss Fitzroy. I take it the dinner party was not to your liking?'

'The seating arrangement was not to my liking.'

'Oh, dear. How was the food, though, because whether or not I will be joining you tonight rests on that?'

He stubbed the cheroot out on the edge of the balustrade and flicked it over the side.

'I've always found that to be a vile habit,' Kitty said.

'Do I possess a single habit that you might not find vile, Miss Fitzroy?'

'None that I'm aware of.'

'Then perhaps I shall light up another one. As there is nothing I could possibly do to please you.'

'You don't need to please me. And we should not be out here together.'

'I'm no danger to you,' he said.

A bell of outrage rang inside of her chest. Mostly because those simple words felt like an indictment against her. As if she were foolish to think even for a second that the beautiful Marquess of Curran could possibly have nefarious designs on plain, loud Kitty Fitzroy.

She was just tired. Tired of being required to participate in these games while it was also clear that no one wanted her here. Not especially.

'Whether I am safe or not is immaterial, as you well know. A dim view would be taken to the two of us being out here without a chaperon. These are the arbitrary rules of the world in which we find ourselves, Lord Curran, whether it makes sense or whether it does not. And I think you and I both know that it does not.'

'Can you keep your voice down, please? Some of us overindulged last night.'

He drew closer to her.

'You are under no obligation to be here speaking to me. So forgive me if I make no consideration for your overindulgence. I am out here because I gave a stirring monologue about the evils of child factory work. And it was not well received.'

He was close enough now that she could see the vague outline of his expression. His blue eyes glinting in the pale moonlight. 'You did?'

'I did.'

'Bloody hell.' He reached into his interior jacket pocket and took out another cheroot. He produced a match along with it, and struck it gamely across the edge of the balustrade, lighting the cheroot and chucking the match away after stubbing it out.

'Don't sound impressed. We both know that you care only for yourself.'

'I do esteem a person willing to put wrinkles in the smooth satin of a well-planned evening, though.'

She laughed. 'You have the right of it. I am a wrinkle. A wrinkle that no one particularly wishes to deal with, and yet here I am.'

'They could use it. A bit of shaking up. They could use being told off.'

'They. You're them.'

'So are you, Kitty,' he said, taking a long drag on the cheroot and blowing smoke to the side. 'You are one of them. The Duke and Duchess of Avondale are your patrons. Your guardians. You will marry a man with a title, even if he is not a duke. Or future duke,' he said, his voice dry. 'You are here, having a Season. A debutante. It is not them. It is us. And so, I suppose we have as much right as any to disrupt if we so choose.'

'At least I do it for a reason.'

He lowered his chin, and his eyes looked nearly black. 'You're so certain that I don't?'

'You have made it quite plain that your greatest ambition is seeking your own pleasure. If I've the wrong of it, you've no one to blame but yourself.'

'That is one thing I like about you. You are quick to tell me that I am due every bit of blame to be heaped upon me. Very few other people call me to account. In fact, the only ones who do are old friends. Who also happen to be peers. So. They are accustomed to calling others to account.'

'Titles mean nothing to me.'

'So on guard. They mean things to those around you, though. So it does not matter what it means to you. As I said, you are as much trapped here as anyone. As much a part of it as anyone. We can disdain it all we wish, but that is the truth.'

'You disdain it?'

It was the first truly interesting thing that Lord Curran had ever said to her.

'I was nine years old when I discovered that my father was a hypocrite, Kitty. And it coloured the way that I saw the world. But rather than pretending that I was better than those around me while indulging my own hedonism, I decided to embrace hedonism, and make a show of it.'

'But this…all of it is a show?' She grappled with that—what he'd said about his father—but didn't quite know what to do with it. Didn't know how much further to press. 'If it's theatre, why bother to participate?'

'Ah, see there is where you and I differ. I feel that if it is theatre, one must play their part. And I play it very well. I am exactly what these people want me to be. I am exactly what they want to see. A disgraceful Claremont. The Marquess of Curran, a lazy, debauched playboy who loves no one and nothing more than he loves his own pleasure, that is the rumour, is that not so?'

'That is…the apparent truth.'

'For those who wish it to be.'

He took another step towards her, and her heart bumped alarmingly in her chest. A warning, obviously. For she knew better than to be out here alone with a man. Any man, least of all him.

That way lay ruination.

She was fuzzy on the details of ruination beyond a brief talking to that she had been given when she had first come to London from the country.

There had been a governess then. And the Duchess of Avondale had charged her with giving Kitty some basic rules about society once she had found out that Kitty was essentially feral and had not been taught the way of things by her father.

You can never under any circumstances be alone with a man.

You could not allow a man any liberties.

Liberties were any touch that extended beyond the kiss of a gloved hand, or the contact of a gloved hand to a gloved hand. If she were promised to be married to the man they could exchange a chaste kiss—that was the word that had been used, *chaste*, and Kitty had puzzled over it and had not known what it meant, but had added it to her vocabulary all the same—on the mouth.

Anything else would mean she was ruined. If she were caught in a position with a man that could be deemed compromising—which it seemed to Kitty was any that involved solitude—she would be unmarriageable. The scandal that would follow would be too great to bear, and she would never be able to recover from it.

But like everything else she had learned about society, she had not truly taken it inside herself. She knew the rule. She just thought it was silly. How was this being ruined? Standing here talking to Lord Curran. He had touched her gloved hand precisely once.

He would never kiss her hand. And he would certainly never kiss her on the mouth—chaste or otherwise.

There was something about that thought that made her skin prickle.

She did not like the man, and he did not like her. Whenever she was done talking to him she felt like a cat that had been picked up and petted backwards, her fur pushed up in an uncomfortable manner. And yet, she couldn't avoid him. He seemed always to be in her path no matter what, and she had no idea why or how that was.

For those who wish it to be...

'And what is the truth?'

'The truth is,' he said, his voice hard, his tone weary, 'the world is broken. You might as well enjoy yourself. Enjoy yourself, Kitty. Do not be so serious. Endeavour to smile.'

'Like when you swept me on to the dance floor against my will?' She ignored the weariness in his tone that made him more of a human, and less of an actor. That made him so much more than the pantomime villain she cast him as in her mind.

'Yes. You might've smiled. Many women would've wanted to be in your position.'

'But I was not among them. So why choose me?'

He hesitated for a moment. 'I don't know. But everywhere I look, there you seem to be. And what am I to make of that?'

She had the distinct impression that he was not a man accustomed to admitting he did not know something. It made her feel as if the terrace had tilted just slightly. 'I don't know. Because everywhere I turn there you seem to be. What am I to make of that?'

'Kitty,' he said, and she noticed then that he was quite close to her. As close as when they had been waltzing. He was not touching her, and yet she could feel the heat from his body.

And something echoed inside of her.

Ruined.

Yes. She had to stay away from ruin. But standing near him felt like something that could not be wrong. It just felt as though it was. As though every single moment she had encountered him was unavoidable, unplanned, and inevitable.

'You want to go back inside,' he said.

'You're meant to be sitting next to me, aren't you?'

He chuckled. 'Yes. But I don't think I will be taking my seat tonight. It was a mistake to come.'

'Why?'

'I am in an ill humour.'

'Why…?'

'It is not your concern. You are not my confidante. We are just two people who happened to be standing out on the terrace at the same time. That is all.'

She felt chastised. And she hated it.

'I know I'm not anything to you. But as I'm not anything to you, perhaps it would be easy for you to unburden yourself.'

She didn't know why she should offer that. He had hurt her. And anyway, she didn't even know why she felt that she knew he was burdened. Only that she did.

'But to unburden myself would be to burden you.

Gravely. And I will not do that, Kitty. You might think me a monster, in fact I'm certain that you do. So allow me to be a gentleman, as I so rarely am, and preserve that which is innocent. Because you are innocent.'

She thought it was a terrible way of describing her. A woman who had lost both of her parents at a tragically young age. A woman who felt beset by the tragedies of the world around her.

How could she be considered innocent in any regard?

'The fact that my saying that puzzles you only proves my point. Go back inside.'

'I cannot. I've made a fool of myself.'

He stubbed the cheroot out. 'Let's go.'

'What?'

'I will accompany you,' he said, his voice hard.

'But won't people know we were alone then?'

'I will simply say that I found you in the hall and escorted you back to the dining room. There will be no trouble.'

Chapter Eight

It was perhaps the only chivalrous thing that George had ever done in his life. He wasn't entirely certain why he was doing it now. Except that Kitty had looked as desolate as he felt, and it was an opportunity for him to remind himself of the part that he had to play.

And there was a part he needed to play. He needed to show his face at the party tonight, and there were very specific reasons why. He had to be here, so it was not suspected he had been anywhere else.

But these games were beginning to wear on him. And after last night…

The image of the little girl, the little girl that he had not been able to get to the doctor in time… That would haunt him for the rest of his life. It would join the many images that haunted him. Because that girl was not singular. Far from it. And that was what made his soul echo with rage.

He was exhausted, and he had not slept. He had discovered the child had no family, and it had somehow wounded him in a way that hurt far worse than if there had been a weeping mother to impart the news to. He felt as if mourning the child was his responsibility, for if he did not she would be forgotten. And yet, he did not have the time. He had to attend dinner parties. And he had more children to save.

And so he took it as another scar to his soul. Because what else could be done?

And in each and every one of these children's faces he saw Hannah. It was always Hannah. And when he failed… When he failed it was an echo that haunted him eternally.

It was why he had to do this. Play this part. Get all the information he could on factories, their practices, the children there.

It went further than child labour. Often the children were taken from there. The ones that disappeared suffering terrible fates in brothels for the sick and twisted.

And he had to know who knew these things. He had to know where these places were. He had to know what the Marquess of Stanton was planning at all times.

And he had to make sure no one suspected him of being the architect of their demise.

But as soon as he and Kitty walked into the house he smiled, for he knew how to do this. He knew it well.

They melted slowly into the foyer, where there were guests mingling, and then on into the ballroom.

'We are seated down there, I believe,' she said, looking at the end of the table with the two empty chairs. Dinner had advanced to its end, with coffee being served.

'Excellent,' he said. 'I do need coffee.'

With a beaming smile he addressed Lady Penelope, the Earl of Wainscott, and Lord Boreham. 'I found this charming creature wandering the halls, and as I was late to this event, she offered to bring me back to my seat.'

'You missed dinner,' Lord Boreham said. 'Shall I tell you what was on the menu?'

'No,' George said. 'I make it a policy to live to regret nothing, and I should hate to regret the glory of this meal. It would be a tragedy that even my rakish soul could not withstand.'

'If you insist,' Lord Boreham responded.

'If only I were able to manage him quite so easily,' Kitty whispered.

George looked at her, her pale face completely void of any colour. She was embarrassed, he could see that, but more than that, she was angry.

That anger echoed in his own soul. He knew it well.

Oh, Kitty. He wished he could have been here for her righteous fury. For her monologue. He imagined that it was a triumph. And it would do these pompous arseholes well to listen. Except they would not. He knew it. It was why he managed things the way that he did.

But Kitty… She possessed no artifice. She simply was.

He had truly underestimated how beautiful she was. Particularly when she was in a fury.

He had seen women in many sorts of temper, but he didn't think he had ever seen anyone—man or woman—in the sort of righteous fury that he often felt burned inside of himself.

He found it stunning.

And she sensed it. He knew. Which was all the more reason to keep her away from him. And yet, here they were. Not away from one another. Yet again.

'I had thought,' Lady Penelope said, 'that you were courting Lady Helene, Lord Curran.'

'She is not in attendance this evening,' he said, stating the obvious.

'Indeed.' Her gaze flickered to Kitty.

Kitty looked bewildered.

She was a funny thing, was Kitty. She smiled so rarely. It felt a personal mission to make her do so. But as he had so many missions, it was one he would have to set aside. Another man would make her smile. And it would be all for the better.

'Well indeed,' said Lady Penelope, casting a sidelong glance at Wainscott, who, George thought, should consider himself warned, but would not, because the man was as thick as building plaster.

He drank the coffee in front of him gratefully. Because he did have a pounding headache, even if it was not from excess.

Lively conversation carried on around them, and he felt as if he was in a different space altogether. He laughed. He did exactly what was expected of him, but he did not feel it. He was caught in the heaviness of it all.

And for the first time he felt as if he were not alone. Because he felt as if Kitty was apart from these people too, regardless of what they had just spoken about on the terrace.

In that moment, he felt as if they were an 'us' and everyone around them was…them.

It was a strange and powerful feeling he had never experienced before and was in no hurry to experience again.

'I must depart,' he said. 'Thank you kindly for escorting me in, Miss Fitzroy,' he said, careful to observe formality. He did not know why. It was so easy to use her given name.

'You're welcome, Lord Curran,' she said, looking confused. Perhaps by the fact that he was being civil. And he supposed he had nothing but his own behaviour to blame for that.

'I shall see you at the next ball, I would wager?'

'As there seems to be no avoiding you, I imagine I will.'

'Perhaps you should save me a dance.'

'Perhaps I shall continue to leave my card at home.'

The piece of him that was the rogue that he pretended to be could not help but take that as a challenge.

Chapter Nine

It was in fact the arrival of Lord Boredom that set her on high alert that evening at the next ball.

It was not the absence of Lord Curran. No, indeed, it was not and could never be that, even if she had spent hours in her room going over and over the conversation they'd had on the terrace as if it were steps to a waltz she had committed to learning well. It was simply because she'd had so few conversations with any one person—not her family—that had lasted so long, and were not entirely one-sided.

She was in her corner.

And that was when she saw him.

But it was also when she saw *him*.

When the Marquess of Curran walked into the room, it was as if everything else went fuzzy at the edges.

It had been happening more and more, that sensation, when he came into her view. But this time, it was quite profound. There was something exceedingly purposeful about the way he moved tonight. He was wear-

ing a black coat with a cream-coloured cravat beneath
it. It was severe, even while fashionable. The way that
his breeches conformed to his figure gave each step
yet more consequence, as did the impact of his shiny
black boots on the ballroom floor. He was not, in that
moment, a man devoid of anything but the pleasures of
life, and the need to pursue them. He was, in that moment, a man of deep circumstance. Forget the pomp.

And it was as if a misty veil had been pulled back,
revealing to her something that she had not seen before.
She thought of that moment a fortnight prior when she
had first thought about the inky depths in those blue
eyes.

He turned his head sharply, and his eyes met hers.
And she felt the impact of it down to her stomach.

And then suddenly, he shifted. Like the sun coming out from behind the clouds, his face gave way to a
grin. Lazy. Indolent. And yet, the burn in his eyes did
not add up.

He did not make his way to her. And it was only then
that she realised she had been standing there quite the
sitting duck while Lord Boredom made his way across
the room.

Damn the Marquess of Curran.

Damn him. Lord Boredom was only a few paces
hence, and she had very little time to decide what to
do. But one thing she knew was that there was a door
only ten paces to the left, and if she slipped through it,
she had a chance of hiding away.

And so she did just that. She ducked so that she was

concealed by the crowd, and slipped through the partially open door. She also closed it slowly and firmly behind her. It appeared to be a library, at least as best she could tell in the darkness. There was no light. She vaguely made out a *chaise longue* in a corner, and she crept on to it, pulling her knees up against her chest as she sat there.

She felt like a silly child playing a game of hide and seek.

But it was easy to scold herself for being unwilling to engage in conversation with a man who might well be harmless if she did not consider the possibility that he might be counting on her to become a candidate to be his wife. She had to be very careful how often she was seen speaking to him, lest Lord Boredom—or anyone else—get the idea that a union between them was an appealing prospect to her. There was only one other person she had spoken to even half as much—

She let that thought break off.

Her speaking to the Marquess of Curran meant nothing. Her dancing with him meant even less.

And everybody had to know that. He was the scandalous darling of the *ton*, and she was the *ton*'s resident brown bird.

He'd been using her in that waltz, and she knew it.

He was all that truly mattered anyway. The scandal sheets were alight with his exploits, and he created such gleeful gossip that he was an absolute favourite of the *ton* to be certain.

She huddled on the *chaise*, and eventually stretched out, lying back.

There were so many books in here, she wished that there was more light. A fire. Something. She had a feeling that it was a beautiful room.

Her mind began to spin with the different books she might find on the shelves.

And before she knew it, she found herself drifting. Drifting off into a dream. Far away from balls. Far away from courtship games. Far away from potential husbands.

And far, far away from George Claremont, the Marquess of Curran.

Tonight was the night. He had everything planned. When he had walked into the ballroom, it had been Kitty Fitzroy that he'd first seen. Standing there against the wall, looking for all the world as if she wished to blend into the wallpaper. As she always did. And yet she had held his fascination. And he had smiled at her. Had forgotten to put on the face of a man who was planning on getting engaged tonight. And he was.

He had decided not to wait for the house party and instead talked to Helene's father just this morning. He was so well practised at looking at men he hated in the eye and smiling.

It would terrify him, were he a different man.

But he was not a different man. He was the man who had decided to destroy this ungodly enterprise and all its offshoots from the inside.

There was a reason he was not active politically.

He had to appear a careless, foolish, selfish playboy. Because men would admit the gravest of sins to such a man.

And George, in perfect character, would laugh as if those sins were antics.

He had once, just two years ago, engaged two men of the *ton* in a bawdy discussion about buying girls who had not yet bled. He went to the police straight after, disguising his identity. Those men were now in jail and no one knew it was all because of George.

And Helene's father, the Marquess of Stanton, facilitated these things, and more. Abuses in factories and out.

Through this connection he could make so much difference.

Tonight, he would propose to Helene.

Tonight, he would take her out to the garden and make the engagement official.

Poor Helene. She was not a girl gifted with the powers of speech. Or indeed thought.

But she was beautiful. And she would be a delight to bed.

She was bubbly and buxom and he had a feeling she knew her way around a man's body.

It would all be well enough in the end.

He did not particularly wish to have a clever wife, when it came down to it. It would not help his cause.

He and Helene would be seen as equals. In looks, in temperament and in interests. Helene was a foolish girl who enjoyed the spoils of profits got by the suffering of others.

She had no idea.

He knew that.

He thought of Kitty. Kitty knew where excess came from.

She was far too clever for any man's good. A wife with that sort of sharpness would do nothing but create endless drama. And he did not need the kind of speculation around him that Kitty would bring, no matter that there were things about her he respected above anyone else he'd met, perhaps ever.

His fate was set. He would not divert from course now.

'Hello, darling,' he said, as he approached Helene.

When he glanced back to the corner, Kitty was gone. Lord Boreham was standing right where she had only just been. He did hope that Kitty had not expired of boredom on the spot. He wondered if her crumpled form might be on the ground somewhere.

A smile tugged at his lips. Only because Kitty herself would have said such a thing, and it would've been amusing.

She was quite acerbic for a wallflower. He wondered if she was aware. It seemed that she genuinely spoke whatever came to her mind, and thought nothing of it. Certainly not of propriety. It was quite charming. As was she, in her way.

Kitty Fitzroy. Charming? He had no idea what the devil he was thinking.

Perhaps it was the looming spectre of marriage that had him thinking such things.

'George,' Helene said, breathless.

She had to know. And she would, of course, be pleased.

He wondered if she would play at being an innocent on their wedding night. He could tell her not to bother. But really, he liked the show. Theatre was such a part of his life. Why deny Helene her opportunity to take part in it?

'I thought we might take a walk,' he said. 'And have a talk somewhere more private.'

'I like that idea very much. But I have it on good authority that the garden here is quite crowded. Perhaps you might meet me somewhere a bit more secluded. The library.'

'The library?' He was truly surprised that she was aware that many houses had libraries. He wondered if she knew how to read. 'You are acquainted with the library?'

She suddenly looked hesitant. And he realised that she had perhaps been in the library of this particular house before, and for nefarious reasons.

'I've been told of it,' she said. 'But there is quite a large one.'

He thought he might know of it. Adjacent to the ballroom. At least, he had seen the door there ajar and the room filled with books.

'I shall meet you there.' She winked. Broadly. It was so obvious and flirtatious.

She wished to give him physical favours, and…the idea made him feel dead. But he was marrying her, and he was not turning back. So he was going to agree. He was going to give her whatever she wanted. And if this was what she wanted on the night of the engagement, then she would get it. If she wished to consummate things now, if she wished to drop to her knees and prove to him what a good wife she would be, then who was he to deny her?

A man with his reputation never would. A man with his reputation likely would've already taken favours from her. He had barely touched her.

But his mind was what was engaged in this pursuit. Not his heart, certainly. And not his body.

So now it was time to make sure to engage the rest of him.

Well. Still not his heart. Never that.

Helene smiled and melted into the crowd. Obviously making an effort to go a separate way than he.

He appreciated her skills at playing the vixen. Though she was perhaps showing more of herself than she would want to show a future husband if that husband was the sort who cared about things like maidenhead. He did not. He had not yet bedded a virgin, and in truth did not care to.

He thought of Kitty Fitzroy.

A woman more certain to be a virgin did not exist.

She was very young. Much younger than he. And even younger in terms of experience.

He wondered if that stern little mouth of hers had ever even been kissed. Likely not.

What would she say if he were to do such a thing? She had been infuriated by his touching of her gloved hand, by him holding her yarn.

He thought of her on the terrace, her eyes closed. She looked in pain even then, as she'd spoken to her father, long deceased.

She'd loved her father, and he'd felt a bigger cad than

he ever had before witnessing that private moment between Kitty and a ghost she loved so dearly.

He had spent his own life in tribute to a ghost, and he knew why you might continue to make vows and speeches to one.

There were times it was all one had.

Kitty understood that.

He ground his teeth together and redirected his thoughts, moving towards the library door. It was shut firmly, which he assumed meant that Helene was already inside.

He pushed the door open and slipped inside, closing it behind him. He could see a pale form draped over the *chaise*, and he felt—impossibly—a slight kick of excitement.

It had been quite a while since he'd indulged himself with a woman. That, he supposed, would be the perk of marriage. He would have ready availability of a woman, in his home, in his bed, whenever he so chose to partake.

He could see, very suddenly, the appeal of that.

He moved over to the *chaise* and sat on the edge. He could barely make out anything, just the pale colour of the ball gown Helene was wearing, and he pushed his hand up beneath to find bare, lovely, smooth legs. She moaned, and rolled on to her back, and he put his hand on her other leg, moving them up higher, the silken glide of her skin beneath his palms intoxicating. He was suddenly ravenous, and what he truly wanted was to go straight for the heart of her and feast.

Perhaps you want to kiss your fiancée before you do such a shocking thing.

And so he found himself moving up the *chaise*, looming over her, and he was poised, ready to lower his head and kiss her, when he realised something.

That was not Helene.

And just then, the door opened, wide. Light spilled in from the ballroom, and there were several shocked gasps.

And there they were. The purported authors of the most popular scandal rag, standing in the entrance, as if it were accidental that the ladies in question had walked into a room that they had just seen him slip into.

'Lord Curran,' one of them said, shocked.

'Lady Balfour.' And that was when he looked back in truth at the woman beneath him, who had frozen like a terrified rabbit. Her eyes were wide, and she was making not a sound, and she had not moved even the barest muscle since that door had opened, so much so, that he had thought her to be dead asleep.

But no. She was awake. And shocked.

As was he.

'Kitty,' he said, his voice hard.

'What have you done?' she asked, suddenly finding her voice. 'What have you done?'

He knew exactly what he'd done. He had succeeded in making a scandal so indecorous that it would be in every scandal sheet, from the most popular to the most obscure, before tomorrow morning. And so, he had no choice. None at all. Because there would be no protecting Miss Kitty Fitzroy from the fallout of this. There was only one thing to be done.

And he could not think right now of how far-reaching the consequences would be.

'I beg your pardon, ladies,' he said. 'You have intruded upon my proposal.'

'Your proposal?' Lady Peregrine asked.

And suddenly they were a light relief of a different kind.

'Miss Kitty Fitzroy has just agreed to marry me.'

Chapter Ten

Kitty was shaking. Trembling. And George had not moved. He was still poised over her, as if he was ready to… And he had one hand still firmly up her dress. It was heavy and rough, which surprised her. That his hands would be rough. He should be wearing gloves, but he was not. His hand was on her bare leg.

His skin was just so very hot. And she had no idea what was happening. To her, around her. She had no idea what to make of any of this.

'I am sorry, of course I did not wish to cause a scandal,' he said, raising a brow, which he knew they could likely scarcely see in the dim light. 'But scandal does seem to follow me wherever I go, even when I'm in the pursuit of respectable life. And of course Miss Fitzroy here will bring an untold amount of respectability to me.'

'Miss Fitzroy,' the women whispered among themselves.

She felt mocked in addition to feeling scalded. She wiggled, trying to get off the *chaise*, but he tightened his hold on her thigh beneath the dress, and a bolt of lightning shot through her. She yelped. Because she had no idea what the feeling was, and she did not like it, and it was centred between her thighs, and it was both foreign and humiliating all at once.

'Do settle yourself,' he said, his face worryingly close to hers. 'There is no need to be upset. All will be well. These ladies know that they have simply encountered what is an entirely explainable moment. We have just got engaged. And nothing untoward has occurred. It was simply that we were looking for some privacy.'

'And a bit of passion,' said the first woman.

'None at all,' he said. 'Really. None at all. Miss Fitzroy is above reproach.'

His hand was still in her dress.

She realised that due to the angle of his body and hers, they could not see that. And he likely did not wish to remove it because if he did it would call attention to it. But it was all she could think of. His hand, her thigh. No other living human had ever put their hand there before. And she was scalded with it. She was wretched with it.

It was the only thing that existed. The only thing.

His fingertips shifted beneath her gown, and she could feel calluses on them.

He had never done a day's worth of work in his life so where had they come from? It was a strange thing to focus on, and yet it was all she could focus on. The texture and quality of his skin. The feel of it against her own. That their temperature seemed to be entirely out of sync.

Oh, yes. And he had just told the biggest gossips in the *ton* that he was marrying her. Perhaps she could think about that for a second, rather than simply the feel of his skin against hers.

'You will have something to write about,' he said. 'The wedding. That I am to be married.'

'Oh, yes,' the women said, and he wondered if they took the warning in his voice.

She was…she was incensed. What was he doing?

'Now,' he said. 'Take your leave.'

The women exited to the ballroom and slammed the door shut, and George looked at her furiously. 'What are you doing here?'

'I must've fallen asleep. I came in because I was avoiding Lord Boredom. What are you doing here? And why did you tell them we were getting married?'

'We were caught in a compromising position, or did you not notice? Your reputation would have been in tatters by tomorrow morning had I not done that. Any hesitation on my part and it would've been irreparably ruined. Those fork-tongued vipers would have written that I had debauched you in a library.'

'I have thought about it,' she said, looking around. 'And I do not think this is the library. It has quite a lot of books, but I came to the conclusion that it is in fact a sitting room.'

'It is not the library?'

'I don't think,' she said.

He let out a vile curse. 'Where do you suppose the library is?'

'I don't know,' she said, sitting up and spreading her hands wide. 'What does that have to do with anything?'

'I was meant to be meeting Lady Helene in the library.'

The starkness of that admission felt like a slap across the face.

Of course. He meant to have his hand up another woman's dress.

'Get your hand off my leg,' she said, humiliation crawling through her. 'It has gone on quite long enough and there is no one here to witness any of this now.'

He slid his hand down her leg, dragging his fingertips along each and every inch. It was uncalled for. Completely and utterly uncalled for.

'I asked Helene's father for her hand in marriage this morning, I will have you know.'

'You must marry her,' she said, misery welling up inside of her.

He wanted to marry another woman. He'd made arrangements to marry another woman. She was a mistake. This entire thing was a mistake. An embarrassing, egregious mistake. And nobody would ever believe it. Nobody would believe that George Claremont had chosen to marry Kitty Fitzroy.

'No one would believe that you intended to compromise me,' she said, her voice low. 'Maybe if I were a different woman that would have to go to such lengths to protect my reputation, but believe me, no one will think that you were so overcome by passion that you had to—'

His face was in shadow, but he was staring at her with the strangest expression. 'Excuse me?'

'What?'

'Is that what you think? That you are in no danger of having your reputation called into question because… because why?'

'I'm not beautiful,' she said, feeling foolish and angry. That he'd made her say that seemed a cruelty too far.

'You think you're not beautiful?'

'I fit effortlessly into a corner.'

'And why do you think men have gone to it to speak to you? You are a debutante, you are—'

'Yes. I'm aware of those attributes. But that is not the same as—'

'You're beautiful, Kitty. Has no one yet told you?'

She felt frozen beneath those words. They did not feel like a compliment. They felt like a sort of death sentence. Perhaps because he sounded so unhappy to speak them. Or perhaps because they lent weight to what he seemed to believe—that they had to marry, else she would be ruined.

'No. No one has said.'

'You are recalcitrant. Your dinner conversation leaves much to be desired, and there is a reason that people find themselves irritated with you. But you are also beautiful.'

'But I'm not… I do not have…'

'Please do not force me to list your attributes.'

But would he? She found herself intrigued by the very idea. She did realise, though, that it was not the best time to have that conversation.

'That aside, Kitty, do not think the *ton* has not noticed our tendency towards finding each other. We were seated next to each other at the dinner party, were we not?'

'You weren't there for most of it.'

'We found one another on the terrace, I escorted you in. I am the only man you have danced with, we have made conversation in ballrooms across London and while we know it is barely civil, does anyone else? Our association is quite fixed in the minds of the *ton*.'

She looked hopeless at the reminder.

'We do not really have to marry,' she said, still scarcely unable to believe what just happened.

'I am afraid that we do,' he said. 'If I do not marry you, my reputation…'

'Your reputation. Your reputation. You're a man. And you have a terrible reputation.'

'Not as a despoiler of virgins, Kitty. There are things a gentleman must never do. And while I might play at being disreputable, I have never debauched a lady. I will not have such rumours starting now.'

'What about the lady that you intended to wed?'

'I intended to marry her. And as such, never took her to my bed.'

To his bed. *To his bed.* She felt utterly incapable of pondering that. What it meant. The implication of it. She did not know what passed between a man and a wife. She needed to speak to Hattie. She needed to speak to Hattie immediately.

'Lord Curran, I cannot…I cannot.' Her breath was coming in short, sharp gasps.

He put his hand on her back, between her shoulder

blades, and she felt instantly…settled. It was the oddest thing. And suddenly, her body began to feel warm. He moved his hand slowly, soothingly, between her shoulder blades. 'It will be well.'

'I don't have money,' she said. 'A very small dowry generously provided for me by the Duke and Duchess of Avondale, but I am not an interest. Not like Lady Helene.'

'Have I asked you for your money?'

She looked up at him. 'No. But everybody knows…'

'I think you will find that everybody does not know. Perhaps not quite to the degree that they think.'

There, shrouded in darkness, she felt as though she had heard the first true thing George Claremont had ever said.

'But we are improbable. We do not know each other. We—'

'Kitty,' he said. 'We know each other as well as any couple who sets an intention for one another during the course of the Season. This is not so unusual.'

'We have nothing in common,' she said. 'You are…' And suddenly, she felt as if she had been jolted out of a daze. Suddenly, she felt access to rage. 'You are the most vapid, shallow, ridiculous man in the *ton*. You make a mockery of everything sincere. You are lazy. You do nothing with your power. Nothing with your privilege. You are the last man on earth that I would've chosen to marry.'

'And yet marry me you will, or no one else will marry you. And then what will happen? I do not think you understand the position you find yourself in. You might as well have given your innocence to me because that is how this will play out, spun into paragraphs of sensationalism in those scandal sheets. They are desperate, hungry to crown society's most scandalous, and you do not want it to be you. It's a lark when it's me, Kitty. When it's you, it's ruinous. You are a woman.'

She did not know how she could give her innocence to a man. And she wanted to ask him how. And what it meant. And yet she felt far too foolish as it was to go and ask such a question.

She only knew it meant ruined. And that ruined in this society meant she would have nothing.

'You will be the wife of a future duke, Kitty. Do you not understand? You will be a duchess one day. Think of what you can do with that. Think of how you can wield your influence. Such good fortune was not to befall you unless something like this occurred. You did not have status enough. And frankly, there are not plentiful enough dukes. This is a remarkable turn of fortune for you, if you can look merely at the title, and not at the man.'

The difficulty was, he was not wrong. He might have been in want of a woman with a dowry now, but when his father died…he would inherit the entire duchy. His political power would be rivalled only by those who carried the same title, and the royal family themselves. It was a position and an opportunity without parallel. A chance to make a difference on a level she had never quite considered.

It rocked her. This realisation.

'And how will we leave here?' Because that was the

first thing that needed to occur. She needed to get out of this study.

'You slip out first. I'll follow.'

'With any luck,' she said, 'people will forget who left first.'

He looked at her blandly. 'That was my thought. If I leave first, then who might come after me will be of utmost interest.'

'You really are so very arrogant.'

'Am I wrong to be? Those ladies did not crash into this room until after they saw me come in. I'm the scandal. But unfortunately, you are now linked to me. Which means you're a scandal yourself.'

And perhaps a duchess. But…he would have to talk to the Duke of Avondale first. And maybe…maybe that would be a way out of it. Right now, she could scarcely believe this was happening.

'There is no time to waste. I will take you home. I will speak to the Duke.'

'Oh. There is no need.'

'There is every need. Because tomorrow, Kitty, your name will be a headline. Unless I want my name to be on a grave marker, it will be best if I make explanation… and an offer…first.'

Kitty stood, stumbling towards the door, and she slipped from the room and out into the brightness of the ballroom. And for one blinding moment she thought perhaps the entire thing had been a figment of her imagination. Perhaps the whole thing had been simply a dream. Perhaps.

Except she knew that the Marquess of Curran had

very rough hands. And she had not known that before she had gone into that room. And she never would've dreamed them that way. She never would've dreamed them on her skin to begin with.

And now, she felt branded by his touch.

She stood there, dazed, in the corner. And then she saw Helene walk into the ballroom, looking vexed.

And Kitty felt an immense amount of anguish towards the other woman.

She had taken the man Helene wanted to marry, and she didn't even want him. How had this happened?

It was then that George slipped out of the room.

'I will ready the carriage,' he said.

And he strode towards the front of the ballroom.

Helene did not go after him. She simply stood, looking like a wax figure. And it was then that Kitty made the difficult decision to follow after him.

Chapter Eleven

Their carriage ride was completely silent. It was a quick journey to the Duke and Duchess's town house and George held his peace during the ride.

This was a disaster.

It upended all of his plans. Dammit. He had been so close to Stanton's factories. To dismantling them. To saving all those children. To…

The access he could have had. To ledgers, to plans. *Dammit to hell.* This destroyed all of it. Kitty offered him nothing in this regard, and worse…she was political and could not keep her mouth shut.

It wasn't the money. It had never been the money. He didn't care at all about that, he didn't need that.

And yet he could still feel her skin beneath his palm.

It enraged him. That she would be so soft. This prickly little walnut of a girl. That she would have skin like an angel designed to tempt a man to sin.

He already knew she had a soul that burned bright enough, and he did not wish to ponder her skin at all.

When the carriage pulled up to the Duke and Duchess's town house, he turned to face her. 'You will go to your room.'

'I will do no such thing. I will be present at the discussion of my fate.'

'You will not, because you will create histrionics.'

'I will not,' she said.

'I am to be your husband, and you will do as I say. I am your lord and master.'

'You…you are nothing of the kind,' she said. 'You accosted me while I slept. I want nothing to do with this. I did not agree to it. And I was promised…that I would not be forced into anything. And yet here you are.'

'It is fate, perhaps,' he said, 'that this has happened. I have been tripping over you all Season. Perhaps it is best if we stop fighting and accept what is.' Except there was absolutely nothing useful in any of it for him.

Of course, for him, marriage had always been an inevitability, not a speculation. But he had always thought that in an endeavour to make the entire farce worth anything he would find a woman who benefited his own ends.

This prickly, improbable creature accomplished none of that.

'I am speaking to your aunt and uncle, whether you follow me into the room or not. And the outcome will be what it is. There is nothing to be done. Nothing at all save moving towards marriage. Do you understand me?'

'What if I refuse?'

'You, darling, are in no position to refuse. If you refuse, you will be at the mercy of whatever the Duke and

Duchess decide. They will not support you for ever. You will not be able to find a position as a governess, not with a scandal like this looming in your background. You are at great peril. You are not the daughter of a duke. You are his niece. Your own father was a fourth son and had gone to rusticate, and he was of no consequence in society.'

'My father was of great consequence,' she said.

The sincerity with which she spoke the words made something in his chest twinge. 'But not to these people,' he said. 'And their opinion is all that matters to them. Your father was odd. You are seen as odd. What will be out there in the world for you if you, a strange girl with very little dowry, ruined by a rake, remain unmarried? What fantasy world do you occupy that this would be a tenable option for you, when you could become a duchess?'

'I don't care about becoming a duchess.'

'And I do not care about becoming a duke. And yet it is the fate that awaits me should my father predecease me.'

'Given your behaviour...'

'Yes. It is a gamble, isn't it? We have no way of knowing for sure who will last. Myself or my father. And yet, we must proceed as if the title will be mine. There are black marks upon my character that I am happy to accept. Black marks that I have earned. But I will not leave you unwed.'

He turned and walked with purpose to the town house, knocking with great force upon the door. She was vibrating beside him. The Duke and Duchess had not attended the night's festivities, and he could only hope that they were not tucked away in their beds. It was the butler who answered the door, and he imagined it was the wide, worried eyes of Kitty beside him that spurred the butler to go and fetch the Duke with such great alacrity.

'I beg you, go to your room, and make this simpler.'

'I will not,' she said.

'When you are my wife,' he said, 'I will pick you up bodily and carry you where I wish to keep you, and deposit you there under lock and key.'

'Well. Now you have given me something to look forward to. And here I thought being your wife was going to be a lifetime of misery.'

'It does not have to be.'

Although, he could not see a scenario where it was not…

He did not love Helene. He wished to use Helene. And he had not yet come up with a way in which to use Kitty.

He pitied her. Looking at her now. Young and pale and she might have been a child next to him. He was only ten years her senior. But she was eighteen. In her first Season. Utterly innocent. And he had no innocence left in his entire being.

He had no use for this tiny, full-of-light creature who possessed not a single shred of artifice. He realised then it was one thing about her that made him uncomfortable.

She had no mask at all. She did not have the understanding of the world deeply ingrained in her to know that she needed one. And she was not protected. He found it disquieting.

Her yarn and her knitting and her endless monologues about the atrocities in the world. It all came from her very heart. As if she had cut herself open so that everyone around could see it. It was not his way. It never would be.

Marrying Kitty felt like bringing the world far too close to his own concerns.

But then, he only needed time. Time to figure out how she might be useful. If there was one thing he was very good at it was making use of those around him as a resource. Because of that mirror.

Except, Kitty did not see him as a mirror. In fact, Kitty saw nothing of herself in him. And wasn't that a true and amusing irony.

The Duke appeared at the top of the stairs, looking… well, not really forbidding at all. But then, that was somewhat his stock in trade.

'Curran,' he said. 'An unexpected visit.'

As it would be. The Claremonts and the Fitzroys did not historically associate.

'I hope you're well,' George said. 'I wish to speak to you, and I did ask that Kitty make herself scarce, but she does whatever she wills.'

'Well, yes,' said the Duchess, joining her husband at the top of the stairs.

'It concerns me,' Kitty said, staunchly. 'And I shouldn't like to be absent when my future is being discussed.'

'I am afraid,' George said, 'that my passions have quite run away with me. And I should have spoken to you before making my intentions known to Kitty, but…well, suffice it to say, there is going to be a bit of a salacious story in the scandal rags tomorrow. But all is well. I intend to marry Kitty.'

The Duke's face went the colour of an aubergine. 'There will be what?'

'He's not compromised me,' Kitty said. 'Not truly. Not really. It was only that we ended up in the same room together by accident…'

'An accident of my proposal of marriage to her.'

'Don't lie,' Kitty said. 'He was intending to have a rendezvous with another woman, and he chanced upon me. I had fallen asleep on a *chaise longue*. And he put his hand up my dress.'

George really did think the Duke might shoot him.

'Thank you for that, Kitty,' he said. 'The truth of the matter is, it does not matter what the truth is. Because we were seen. By the writers of said scandal sheet. Whether or not it was my intention to propose to Kitty is now immaterial. We will have to marry else her reputation will be compromised beyond redemption. And I will not pretend that I am a mere victim of circumstance, not when my own reputation plays a part in the interpretation of what was seen.'

'Oh, dear,' the Duchess said.

'You do not have an attachment to him, Kitty?' the Duke asked.

'No,' she said.

'It does not matter,' George said. 'You are a reasonable man,' he said to the Duke of Avondale. 'A rational man. You know that the only thing that matters is what was seen. Not what is true. Truth is not what is printed, truth is not action. We are men of rational thought. And we both know this to be true.'

'Curran, I...'

'What? You do not wish to force your niece into a marriage against her will, I comprehend that. You also do not wish to consign her to a life of spinsterhood.'

'The scandal...'

'I don't care about scandal,' Kitty said, the boldness of ignorance on full display.

'Because you are a child,' George said, losing his temper now. 'I cannot marry Helene, not after that. It would disgrace her, as well as you, as well as me. I am to take a wife this Season, and though I would not have chosen you, this is the measure of it.' He turned and looked at the Duke. 'I trust you will see the sense in it.'

George realised that this entire moment was a mask slip. George Claremont, as known by every person in this room, possessed not one bit of intensity quite like what he had evinced in these past moments.

But it was all a distraction. And he resented it. He did not wish to play games. He did not wish to engage in negotiations with a girl who did not have the good sense of self-preservation.

'I understand you, Curran,' said the Duke. 'And of course, I will consent to the marriage.'

'Your Grace...' Kitty began.

'He is to be a duke,' Avondale said. 'A duke, Kitty. You will not do better. And if you do not marry him, and the story runs in the scandal sheet tomorrow, you may not marry at all. You will be by yourself. You will have nothing. No one will wish to marry you, and he is correct, his reputation is a catalyst for these events. Were he a man of honour, then perhaps it could be explained. But a rendezvous with George Claremont in a darkened room can only ever be perceived as one thing. What is written about it will be what becomes the truth of it. I will not feed you to those wolves. You do not understand. You are not from London. It is not your way.'

'Why is it the way? Why is it the way of it all?'

'Because it simply is, Kitty,' said the Duchess. 'We do not make the rules, but we must live by them.'

'I thought we were the scandalous Fitzroys, ever thumbing our noses at tradition. I thought… And you,' she said, rounding on him. 'You are supposed to be the most scandalous man in the *ton*. Why are you so bound to honour now?'

'Because there is an art form to skirting the edges of propriety,' he said. 'And I believe that the Fitzroys will agree with me. You do not push them so hard that they break. For if they break, the entire structure collapses around you, and you cannot withstand the results of that. Believe me.'

'Shall we procure a special licence?'

'A special licence will only reinforce the idea that something untoward did occur,' George said. 'I've no interest in special licences. We will have the banns read.'

'That is a bold move,' the Duke said.

'I am happy to maintain that whatever was seen was simply my proposal. We were alone together, but…'

'They did not see that he had his hand up my dress,' Kitty said.

'Thank you, Kitty,' he bit out. 'Naturally, had that been seen, we would be having a different discussion regarding special licences.'

'You are a Claremont. You would have no trouble procuring one,' the Duke argued.

'It is not about the trouble. It is about the view.'

'I appreciate that. But perhaps you should wait and see what the scandal rags write before you are quite so definitive,' the Duchess suggested.

George relented there. 'Yes. Our actions will need to be dependent upon the gossip.'

And suddenly, Kitty let out a cry of alarm, and went racing up the stairs. Past her aunt and uncle, then down the hall.

'Will she be all right?' the Duchess asked her husband.

'I don't know,' the Duke said. 'But her reputation will be preserved as best as we can.'

'It is an unfortunate turn of events,' George said. 'Believe me, I take no joy in them.'

'Perhaps you had better stop looking like a man on his way to the gallows,' the Duke said. 'My niece did not choose to marry you. And in my opinion, you are the architect of this disaster. You will not harm her any more than you already have.'

'I have no interest in harming your niece. What I do is to protect her.'

'Then see that you do, Curran. See that you do.'

Chapter Twelve

Kitty was in misery, and could not be roused the next day. Not until Hattie appeared at the house, with much grave concern.

'How bad is it?' Kitty asked, eyeing her friend warily.

'It is all over the scandal sheets.' Hattie regretfully took a folded paper from her reticule. 'See for yourself.'

Kitty took the paper from her and unfolded it.

Scandal at the ball, where Miss Kitty Fitzroy was caught in a compromising position with none other than the Marquess of Curran, who has now declared that they are to be wed. A love match, or a hasty attempt to cover a salacious rendezvous...?

'There was nothing salacious about it,' Kitty protested.

'I believe you,' Hattie said. 'Though...do you mean to tell me there is no connection between you and George Claremont? Only it seems to me that you are quite heavily concerned with his behaviour.'

'There is no connection between us,' she said, her voice rising a pitch. 'None. I was sleeping on the *chaise longue*, and he came into the room… He thought I was another woman. He does not care about me.'

She realised that it wasn't even the most upsetting part of it. 'He doesn't care about anything at all. Not about anything that I esteem.'

'But you will be his Marchioness. And some day a duchess. You will have influence over society. This is what you've always wanted, Kitty. You can marinate in your unhappiness, or you can take it for what it is. You have been given a gift.'

Kitty thought about that long and hard for the rest of the day. But she still did not leave her bedchamber. Not until the arrival of George Claremont, Marquess of Curran, was announced.

'I don't wish to see him,' she said to her maid.

'I do not think it was a request,' the maid responded. 'Now, be of good cheer,' she said. 'He's very handsome.'

He was. And Kitty still had no idea why that ought to matter so.

She supposed because she had to look at the man every day for the rest of their lives.

Heat pricked her eyes. Anguish pulled at her soul. She let her maid dress her in a gown of gossamer silver, and she was certain the gown was new, as she had not seen it before, and her consternation only grew. How was she to survive this? A life of excess that would surely be part of her everyday living with him. How would she retain what mattered?

You have influence.

But George seemed not to exercise any of the influence that he had. And how would she be able to… stand that?

Perhaps you can reform him…

There was no reforming a man like him. There would have to be one notch in the hard, smooth wall of his impenetrable soul to find purchase, and yet, there was nothing.

She exited her bedroom and went down the hall, coming to a standstill at the top of the stairs. She looked down and saw him there, in the hall, an exquisitely fine figure in a grey coat this afternoon.

She tried to do a mental calculation on how much it might have cost, but her brain stalled looking at the set of his broad shoulders and tripped over itself. As if it had clumsy feet. And suddenly she found herself admiring the tailoring of the garment. The way it conformed to his masculine figure, so different than her own.

Why were men so different? They were nearly like a different species. So large and broad. He, in particular, looked as though he would be inestimably solid. As if he himself were a wall of granite. Her heart began to beat faster. She looked down at his hands, gloved now. But she remembered when they had been bare, and pressed against her thigh.

She remembered also when that same hand had held her yarn out to her. That little crimson ball pooled there in the centre of his palm. She snapped back to the moment.

'I regret to inform you that I feel as if we must obtain a special licence,' George began.

'But you just said last night…'

'I did,' he said, his voice terse, 'but that was before the scandal sheets came out this morning, and before I went to the gentleman's club this morning. There are bets on the books as to whether or not you are with child. The gossip among the men is ever so much worse than the gossip among the women, because it does not even have the edge of concern to it. It is simply about whether or not I have been up your skirts.'

'Well, you have been,' she said, feeling in a daze.

'That is not what I mean.'

'What do you mean?' They were still shouting with stairs between them.

'Come down here,' he said.

'I…'

The housekeeper came in. 'Oh, my. Should you not wish to be in the sitting room, my lord?'

'Yes,' he said. 'We shall take tea.'

The way he ordered around members of a household that was not even his own set her teeth on edge, but she followed him into the sitting room and perched on the edge of the chair. 'What do you mean up my…'

'Kitty, we have not time. I have spoken to the Archbishop of Canterbury about a special licence.'

'Oh.'

'I expect that we will have it in two days' time. And we will marry as soon as possible.'

'We do not even know each other,' she said.

'I did not know Helene Parks. We had shallow conversations in a ballroom. It matters not. It is not about knowing one another.'

'What is the purpose of marriage?'

'Children, I should think. Pedigree, and the continuation of a bloodline.'

'The Fitzroys and the Claremonts…'

'Yes. It is nearly enjoyable in its perverse twist, isn't it? To join the two families together even more closely. Almost wish it would have been by design.'

'I am sorry. Did you care for Lady Helene?'

He appraised her slowly. 'No. I do not care for anyone, Kitty. Not anyone but myself. I do not wish for you to walk into this union not understanding fully that which is occurring.'

She nodded slowly, the back of her throat aching. 'I understand.'

'I am not certain you do.'

'Lord Curran…'

'George. You will call me George. And I will call you Kitty. And we will be married in two days' time.'

'But I was supposed to have a couple of Seasons. I was…' And she suddenly felt so very aware that she was being plucked away from her own life, yet again. She had lost every security, every certainty after her father had died. And that was after she had lost softness and the impression of the feminine with the death of her mother when she'd been so young. She had found a little niche for herself with her aunt and uncle. And while her debut had signalled something new, she thought she would have time to get used to what was ahead. Now she was just…being wrenched away from this place. From what she had carved for herself here. A new house, a new…everything. It would be entirely different, being his wife.

Being a wife at all.

She had wanted time. Time to grow accustomed to the change of it. But no. There would be none of that.

She felt wretched.

'You needn't worry,' he said. 'I'm not a beast.'

'I don't know what it means to be a wife,' she said, beseeching now.

'I am certain the Duchess will enlighten you.'

'Will she?'

'She certainly can.'

'Why hasn't anyone enlightened me until now?'

'Because you were not engaged to be married before now.'

She felt deeply uncertain about all of this. About everything. She felt precarious. In the most deeply real way.

'Good day,' he said.

He got up and tipped his hat.

'Will you be speaking to my uncle?' she said.

'I will send a missive later. Your family may attend the wedding, of course. But we will keep it small.'

'Yes,' she said, choking on the reply.

Until this moment, in many ways, Kitty had felt very much a girl. And suddenly, she realised that she was a woman. With the concerns and cares of one. But no education about what it meant.

And she felt desolate.

Two days. All she had was two days. Then her world would change for ever.

Chapter Thirteen

'Congratulations are in order, I am to understand?'

He looked at Lily Bell's face. 'Yes,' he said. He would be married to Kitty in less than two days.

'I thought you were seeking a union with the Parks girl.'

'I was.'

'And?'

'We both know you read the scandal sheets, Lily Bell. I do not think you need actually hear the story from my own lips.'

'Such fine lies they are, George. Why don't you take this opportunity to weave me a pretty lie?'

'I won't,' he said. 'Though the truth of it is that it was simply a misunderstanding. A misunderstanding that will now become a marriage.'

'I do not understand the games you aristocrats play. If you do not wish to marry someone, then why do it? If I had power, status, and money, I would do what I please.'

'You already do what you please.'

She shrugged a shoulder. 'True. But I do it in the shadows. And wouldn't it be a nice thing, to not have to live in them simply because my actions have been deemed unwholesome?'

'It is the way of things.'

'And the people with the power to change those things refuse to do it.'

'What do you think I'm about?' He looked at the woman full in the face. 'Why do you think I do any of this?'

'I don't know, George. I have asked myself why you do these things for a very long time. I can't seem to figure it out. I had thought that perhaps...'

'I'm sorry,' he said. 'I am sorry if I gave you an expectation that I could not fulfil. That was never my intent.'

'I know. Whether or not the whole rest of the world is aware of it, George, I actually know that you are a good man.'

'I try not to be a bad one.'

Or at least, he made an effort to try to unpick some of the horrendous actions put in place by those like him, and...anything his existence did to support the kind of vile behaviour that he actively worked against.

Whether he was good or bad would be for God to judge. He had blood on his hands. But the blood was not innocent.

Still, who among them was righteous?

He worked to rescue those who were innocent. That was all he could be proud of.

'I take it you will not be to visit for a while?'

'No. It will likely not be possible. I will need to re-consider some things. But that was always going to be the case. If I married Helene, similar changes would've had to occur. There just would've been more time.'

'I understand.'

'The house, everything here…it will remain the same.'

'Thank you, George. For the assurance.'

'You will not find yourself out on the street. None of you will.'

'I trust in you. Please don't disappoint me.'

'Never.' He put his hand over hers for a moment, and then took it away. He was to be a married man soon. And he thought of the way that Kitty had looked up at him. Beseeching.

I don't know what it means to be a wife.

A kick of something that felt quite a lot like lust burst in his gut like a powder keg.

It was unconscionable, unreasonable that her admission of such deep innocence should spark anything other than disgust in him.

And yet, there had always been something about Kitty that compelled him. He could not deny it. It mattered not. If she did not receive an education from the Duchess, she would get a brief, practical bit of instruction from him. On their wedding night.

He ignored the heat that flared in his gut at that thought.

Theirs was not to be a marriage of passion. It was one of convenience. And he could not afford to be distracted by passion, so it would remain that way.

* * *

It was the day of the wedding, and what surprised Kitty the most was how usual everything felt. She woke up in her bed, as expected, and while she was put into a lovely gown, it was nothing overly remarkable. It wasn't until she was sitting downstairs with the Duchess, awaiting the moment when the carriage would be brought up front, and they would all leave, that she began to understand that today truly was not like other days. Wildly, she met eyes with the Duchess of Avondale. 'I do not know what it means to be a wife,' she said.

'Oh,' said the Duchess. 'But you are from the country. Surely you have…surely you've seen… You see, Kitty, when… Animals. Horses. Perhaps you have seen horses about the business of appropriation?' The older woman looked a bit pale.

'No,' Kitty said. 'I've not. And I do not see what that has to do with being a wife. I am not a horse.'

'No. Dear. Indeed you are not. Of course not. It is only that you might have found it an instructing reference point.'

'I do not,' Kitty said.

'Kitty…what happened exactly between yourself and Lord Curran when you were found in the library?'

'He sat on the edge of the *chaise*, he slid his hand up beneath my skirt, and he was very close to me. As if he was about to kiss me.'

'You understand kissing,' her aunt said.

'I know what it is.'

'It is that. It is that…but more. And he will know all there is to know.'

'He will know.'

'Yes.'

She began to spottily draw lines between these things. The things that men were allowed to do, the ways in which they moved rather freely, versus the ways that her movements and the movements of other young ladies were quite restricted.

'He knows these things because he is allowed to do what he wants?'

'Yes.'

'Has he learned them from reading?'

'Kitty…'

'Well, he has no children. So how…?'

'Kitty, you do not need to know all of the details. George will explain them. And if he does not explain them, you can at least trust that he will act in a responsible manner to ensure that…the act is well and truly understood by at least the end of the first week.'

'A week?'

She was more confused than when she had asked the question.

Why would George know? Why could she not be told now? Why was everyone in London so desperately pleased with how clever they were, when they were afraid of so great many topics? It was as though they were both terrified of and obsessed with all interactions between men and women. She could not say for sure, but she did not think things were half so confusing in the country.

'It does not seem to be a terribly practical manner of conducting marriage. Or indeed the world. And if these men—these titled men—are in possession of so much power, why did they not construct a more suitable, sensible system?'

The Duchess of Avondale let out an exasperated breath. 'Because this benefits them. They have no reason to examine a different way of doing or being because this way works for them.'

She had a feeling that that was the most honest answer she had been given during the course of this conversation. And it made the most sense. Of course it benefited the men. It must somehow. Though, George did not seem overly pleased with much of any of it.

Too soon, it was time for her to bundle up in the carriage, and she was no more educated on the facts of being a wife than she had been before she had sat down with the Duchess. Though she did feel a touch more understanding of the way of the world. Oh, not more accepting of it. In fact, if anything, she felt as though she had been cut clean through with a blade of cynicism, slipped unerringly beneath her skin. The world was as it was because those in control stood to gain from the way it was structured. It was not a flaw in the system, rather it was designed this way. To hurt the vulnerable. To control those who otherwise had no power of their own.

To use them as playthings.

What a thing to be stewing on as she made her way to her own wedding. And yet, she could think of nothing more intrinsically her. Except…

She reached into her reticule and pulled out her knitting.

'I do not think you need to make any socks today,' the Duchess said.

But she was filled with fiery conviction.

'I need to make socks today more than I have ever needed to make socks,' she said.

'If you must,' the Duchess said.

And Kitty was confident that she must.

The drive to the church was not a long one. Sweet Annie and Kitty's aunt and uncle were present, as was Hattie and her husband, the Earl. It was otherwise a small affair. And she was somewhat surprised to see that neither George's sisters Felicity and Dorothea, nor his father and mother were in attendance. She had not yet made the acquaintance of the Duke and Duchess, and she had expected to do so today.

She did not see George. Perhaps the groom had not bothered to show up to the wedding. It would rather make the issue of his parents' lack of attendance seem moot.

But then, suddenly there he was. She knew that the coats he wore were different, though there was little variance between them, but somehow today the black of his jacket seemed darker, the white of the shirt yet more pristine. His figure was severe. And in that moment, she saw the man she had seen cutting his way through the ballroom the night of her eventual ruination. The same man who had spoken to her aunt and uncle about marrying her. The man who possessed an overabundance of determination, and not one ounce of foolishness. The man who seemed to stand in direct opposition to the one the world imagined George Claremont to be.

'Let us be done with it then.'

The priest, who seemed nonplussed by the entire event, took his position. It did not matter to him that those in attendance were baffled, and that the bride seemed bewildered. That the groom was angry if anything.

Kitty imagined that these were the sorts of weddings had in society all the time.

In fact, it seemed very like it was designed to be so.

What an epiphany.

The priest recited vows from the book of common prayer as they took hands.

His hands.

They had been on her before. And it was only the touch of his hands now that kept her from rising from her body and surveying the scene like a ghost.

Hot. Rough. Masculine.

Familiar, to her chagrin.

They rooted her to the spot. Grounded her in the moment.

And part of her, a small part that was crouched inside of her, shaking its fist, demanded to know when she had become such a coward that she would succumb to this indignity. The truth of the matter was, she was not being forced. No one was holding her here against her will. She could not claim that. She ached with that reality. She was choosing this because it was the path of least resistance. Because he had made his case—without this marriage she would be ruined. And because it was clear the Duke and Duchess expected it of her.

And because of what he had said to her about her own influence.

It galled her to admit that. But the truth of it was, the world was designed to benefit those with titles and masculine features. She could not fashion herself into a man. But she could style herself as a marchioness. Something she had never aspired to. But now she had a mission—a point and a purpose—and it was so much bigger than herself, and so much bigger than the morsel of power she had been given upon her entry to this world, she had to take what increased influence might be afforded to her. She would not be a future duchess who simply knitted socks in a circle. She could not wholly condemn the Duchess of Avondale; she only knew what she knew.

But Kitty also knew what she knew. And it burned bright within her as a conviction.

What a lonely thing. To be married to a man who thought nothing of these things at all.

George recited his vows, his voice deep and sure, and when she looked into his blue eyes, she felt something begin to expand in her chest. How could you speak such words to a stranger? She didn't understand, and yet she had just done so, and he had done so in return.

And so, they were presented there before their guests as man and wife, the deed done just like that. Vows she could not even find resonance to inside of her soul, and a piece of legal paperwork. That was all it took to bond you to a man for life.

She was his now.

And she would never be her own again.

You have never been your own. Such is the plight of a woman in this world.

And there were many others who were worse off than she, for at least those who had ownership of her took care. She would not feel sorry for herself. Not when she had just married a titled, coveted man. She might never have coveted him herself, but it mattered not. She would waste not a moment of pity on herself. Not any more. For now she had resources and with them she would… Did they have resources? She imagined that as his wife she would get an allowance. And as far as she knew, he had an allowance. But she did have a dowry, so there was that. They would have that. But maybe he would squander it. Maybe nothing would be given to her. Maybe she had gained absolutely nothing.

But some day you will have the entirety of his family inheritance.

And if she knew one thing about the Claremonts it was that they were exceedingly wealthy and influential. Would he take his father's seat in the House of Lords? And if he did, could he be persuaded to champion her causes?

While she was thinking these things, her aunt pulled her in for a hug. 'Remember, you will be all right.'

She sounded as though she was sending her off to war.

Hattie pulled her in for a hug as well. 'Don't worry.'

'That is not reassuring,' Kitty whispered.

Hattie took her hand and dragged her away from the knot of people. 'When the time comes. When he takes you to the marriage bed, tell him that you do not wish him to be quick. Tell him you wish it to be pleasurable.'

'Hattie…'

'Tell him,' Hattie said, nodding with an intensity to her gaze that gave Kitty nothing more than a mental notebook of further questions. And then she found herself being ushered out the door, towards a shiny black closed coach that was clearly her husband's, for all that it was imbued with an ostentatious flair and untold majesty.

Just like the man himself.

'We are on the way to my town house,' he said once they were alone.

She suddenly wondered how near his town house was to that of his mistress. Men kept mistresses. To do what with? She did not know. She would know the answers to all these questions tonight, she had a feeling. All tangled up in procreation—and horses? And pleasure.

The word made an uncomfortable ache begin to spread through the lower part of her stomach.

She looked at her husband, who sat beside her in the carriage.

Her husband.

Her husband.

She kept trying the word. Turning it over. Looking at it from different angles. It seemed so foreign. It seemed so improbable.

Her husband.

Hattie had said to ask him…but not now. When he took her to bed. The marriage bed. His bed? Bed.

Kitty was not stupid. She had done a great amount

of reading. But the topic of marriage had not been part of her reading. Her father certainly hadn't had anything on the subject in his library, and the Duke and Duchess hadn't either. At least, not in any place where she had found it.

She had needed a couple more years in the ballroom. There she would've overheard things. She would have learned more. Mating. She had mentioned mating to Hattie and received the scolding. She knew it meant for animals to pair up, and that it also meant to procreate. She simply didn't know of all the details in between. And this was the problem. She had a fair understanding that the details in between would be very, very important to her as the evening wore on.

Why did she not feel changed? She didn't want to feel changed, but she had had some sort of expectation that becoming a married woman would…that she would feel something for the man sitting beside her. But she felt like he was a piece of rock. The face of the mountain. A beautiful one, it was true. But she did not know the way through the wall. And there was a wall.

'George,' she said, testing his name out.

He turned to look at her. 'Yes.'

'George, I…' And she thought she ought to try again. 'I do not know how to be a wife.' She said it beseechingly.

'The Duchess did not enlighten you?'

She shook her head. 'She said that you would know. That you would know all that was required. But I don't understand how.' He looked at her with an expression of alarm. And she realised that she had succeeded in shocking this man. At another time she might've celebrated that as a victory, that she, the champion corner dweller of the Season, had shocked society's most scandalous. At least, he was well on the road to becoming society's most scandalous. He would definitely have won had he not married her.

And suddenly, without warning, he leaned across the expanse of the carriage, and cupped her chin in his hand. 'Let us start at the beginning.'

And then he pressed his mouth to hers.

Chapter Fourteen

She knew about kissing. Of course. She had seen any number of chaste kisses pass between the Duke and Duchess since moving into their home.

This was not…chaste. She could say that with confidence, even with her limited understanding of all things that passed between men and women.

This was *not chaste*.

His lips were firm and hot, and he angled his head, forcing her lips apart, and she felt the slick breach of his tongue.

She had the dim thought that she ought to be horrified. That she ought to be disgusted. And yet suddenly the fact of his fine figure and overall beauty made sense. For it was the reason that she did not recoil. It was the reason that she let out a small whimper and softened beneath the shocking invasion.

His large rough hand cupped her cheek—why was his hand so rough?—and his mouth moved over hers, moving deeper and deeper each time. She trembled, and she wondered if she was supposed to be mimicking his movements. If she was supposed to respond in kind.

She startled, and then did, and found the tip of her tongue brushing against his. And he groaned, a masculine sound that reverberated inside of her, that seemed to echo between her legs in a most embarrassing place. And it was like beginning to see. Beginning to understand.

He moved away from her abruptly, his withdrawal as shocking as his initial advancement.

'That is the beginning.'

'Oh,' she said. 'And there's more?'

He looked at her, and there was no mask over his face, and it was clear that he was at the end of something. A muscle in his jaw jumped.

'Yes. There is more.'

'And you will… We…'

'What do you know of intercourse?'

The word conjured up nothing but a blank space in her mind. 'I don't.'

Her cheeks went warm, and she knew she needed to say what Hattie had instructed her to say before she lost her nerve. 'But I would like it to be pleasurable, not fast.' She hoped that she was using it in the proper context.

His face turned to stone. 'You know nothing, and yet you know to ask me this?'

'Hattie told me to say it.'

He laughed. 'Of course she did. And God love Beaufort. Clearly he is providing a service to the new Countess.'

She didn't understand, and she found it made her very angry. 'I do not like being made fun of.'

'How are you being made fun of?'

'Everyone knows what is to become of me tonight except for me.'

'Would you like me to explain to you, in detail?'

'Yes.'

'I don't know that you would.'

'Yes, I would. I wish that everyone would stop telling me what I want. And that what I want to understand I don't actually want to understand. Perhaps it is enough for the Duchess to say that you will show me. But it isn't. Not for me.'

'Of course not, Kitty, because you cannot do the expected thing, can you?' He looked vexed. 'You simply refuse to be the expected thing, do you not?'

'I have never wanted to be expected. What I wanted was for my life to go on being as it was. And then, when I was sixteen, my father died, and my whole world became something I no longer recognised. And everything that I was supposed to want was taken and twisted. I had thought that I would marry some day, but I had the expectation of meeting a boy in the village, of getting to know him, and taking walks. Of eating dinner with him and my father. Taking tea in our little country house, and then I moved here and it became a game—a game to which I do not know the rules—and I found out that the world was cruel. Not only did it take my mother from me, but it took my father as well, and I came to this city where it seems as if the dirt in the air blocks out the sky, and perhaps that is why it sometimes feels as if the people have forgotten God and goodness and charity. In the pursuit of what? This…this game that has been created where people are moved around as pieces on a board, and for whose amusement? Whose benefit? We are written about in scandal rags as though we are characters in a horrid novel, and this is supposed to be real to me? And then I am simply supposed to march upstairs to…the marriage bed, and trust that you will know what to do. And trust that it is sufficient that you do. I do not trust it. And I will not accept it. I will not relent. I wish to know. I do not have to be ignorant. Even if I must be your wife.'

He stared at her, his expression hard. 'You're not wrong. There is an absurdity to this. To the fact that tupping is the primary thing most members of the *ton* are concerned with. Who is, who isn't, and when they might next. And yet, for the debutantes, little must be known about it, as your innocence must be protected. But if you are found to be in a compromising position with a man—though you may not fully understand what constitutes a compromising position—your entire life will be ruined. You are correct. The rules of society do not make sense. And so, you are also correct, why should you not know?

'The act can be used for procreation, of course. It is the way it is done. But to diminish it to procreation alone removes the truth of it. We are all driven by this need. Once you discover it, you will understand. There are ways to engage in the act, and not cause a woman to be with child. And believe me, most of the *ton* is in no way acting with propriety where this is concerned.'

'It is another game. Another game with rules that only certain people are held subject to.'

'Yes. I can explain the act to you as if I were explaining to you how to waltz. You remember when we waltzed?'

'Yes,' she said.

'I could explain to you the mechanics. But would it capture the way it feels as you move to the music? The way that it feels when I hold you in my arms, and we glide across the dance floor as if we are propelled by something other than mere steps? There is magic in the dance, isn't there?'

She nodded, feeling scratchy.

'So then to describe to you the act that occurs between a man and a woman in bed in mechanical terms would give you some understanding. But it would not let you know what it feels like to dance. And in that way, my kiss likely informed you of more. What do you feel?'

'What do I feel?' She felt small and frightened all of a sudden.

'From the kiss.'

She felt alight with embarrassment, and she wasn't even entirely sure why.

'Go on. Your breath became more shallow, the colour was heightened in your face. Your pupils became wider. Your eyes darker as a result. An indication to me of your desire.'

'My desire.'

'To be closer to me. That is what the act is. If a kiss is appropriately given, then it will make you want to be closer. And you will remove any barrier to get there. Clothes being a primary barrier.'

She thought of the way his hand had felt against her thigh again.

'And then you will want to be closer still. As close as two people can be. You will be driven mad by the need of it. The weight that you begin to feel in your breasts, the tightness in your nipples. The ache between your legs. The slickness there.'

She felt as if she was on fire. For how did he know these things? How did he see them? It had been a kiss, and he had not touched her in any of the places that he spoke of now, and yet he knew. Could describe the symptoms created by the kiss with unerring accuracy.

Was it all women who felt this when a man kissed them? Or was it that his body felt the same?

'Is your body similarly afflicted?'

He looked up, as if he were beseeching the heavens for something, and then he took hold of her hand and pressed it against his lap. He was hard there, and entirely different than she. She had seen statues, she knew that male anatomy was different, but this bore no resemblance to what she had seen on those statues. She had rather thought that those statues looked as though men had a dangling fake between their legs.

But that was not what she felt now.

'Our bodies are designed each to fulfil a specific function. Men to take. Women to receive. I grow hard. You grow wet.'

'I see.' She was trembling now. All of the disquiet she'd ever felt around him seemed as if it had gathered in her stomach, and had become a collective.

So overwhelming she could scarcely breathe past it.

'And I will not ask this of you tonight.'

The carriage stopped then, in front of his town house.

'You won't?'

'No. I will not.'

'But…'

'I have other matters to see to tonight. You have no need to worry. I will not demand that which you are obviously not prepared to give.'

For some reason, it made her ache. For some reason, it made her feel heartbroken. And she had no reason at all to feel that way.

God in heaven. She was so innocent. It killed him. He wanted to take her up against him and show her exactly what he wanted to do with her. He had wanted to tell her, in yet more graphic detail, exactly what pleasure could be found between the two of them in the marriage bed.

But she was terrified, and he could not…

It was best if he removed himself from her vicinity.

He would go visit Lily Bell tonight.

She wasn't expecting him, hell, he had told her not to expect him. But he could not…he could not force his attentions on his trembling bride.

It was all a disaster. What a time to discover that he possessed a particular conscience.

He could've made her desire him.

But the truth was, he did not…he could take no joy in that.

He knew that she had been safely installed in a room adjoining his, and that his staff would take adequate care of her. He dressed, putting on a dark cloak, and asking his valet to have his carriage prepared. He preferred to travel in a closed carriage, because he preferred not to be witnessed on certain nights.

Under the cover of darkness, he left the house, and took the familiar journey to Lily Bell's town house.

'Go to the back,' he said to his man as he got out. Then he walked up the footpath, where Lily Bell opened the door.

'I was not expecting you tonight.'

'I know.'

'You're a married man now. Shouldn't you be entertaining your wife?'

He laughed. 'My wife is so innocent she looked as if she was about to be set upon by a wolf. I found I had no stomach for it.'

'Really? I would've thought a man of your reputation would enjoy such a challenge.'

'We both know my reputation does not tell the whole story. Now. Tell me how many are in residence at the moment.'

Lily Bell looked as if a change had come over her. 'There are eight. Three boys, and five girls. We are working to find a place for them. Their families cannot afford them if they don't work, but the conditions of the factory are killing them. There's a boy, particularly… his lungs are not strong. And what they breathe in at the factories…'

'I know. I'm well aware.'

'One girl was just released from the hospital.' Lily Bell's face twisted. 'She does not have hands. I do not know what will become of her, but her family will not take her back.' Tears welled in her eyes. 'You know what they would have done to her. Hands or not they'd have had her making money on her back. She's eight, George.'

His stomach turned. 'She must go to the country home.'

'Do you think your father will ask questions?'

'He won't notice. She will go to the country home as a hire, but… You know how I intend for it to be run. If you can find a family that will consent to have her live with them, cover the costs?'

'Yes, my lord.'

'Thank you.'

'Are you going out tonight?' Lily Bell asked.

'Yes. I've heard about working conditions at one of the factories. Extremely unsafe.'

'You are risking a lot.'

'Yes. I don't regret it.'

'And if you're found, the likelihood that you'll be arrested…'

'The terribly sad thing is I'm not certain that I would be. Angry merchants accusing a future duke of…sabotage?'

'And do you have plans for what will become of the children when they have no jobs?'

'Yes. I have made careful note of all who have jobs there, and I will figure it out.'

'It's a good thing that your imports have been successful, but of course your strict requirements about the goods you take limits what you're able to make.'

'Indeed it does. If the entire world cared just a bit about where their goods came from, that wouldn't be the case. But sadly, that change is far from coming into effect. I'm aware of my limitations. But I will continue to work as hard as I can. Do not worry, Lily Bell.'

'I'll never forget her either, you know.'

He nodded. 'I know.'

'For what it's worth…you made a difference in my life.'

'If only it hadn't been too late for Hannah.'

And with that, he went through the town house and out the back to where a horse was waiting for him. He would not take a carriage. He put the hood of his cloak over his head. And he rode like the devil to the factory district.

Chapter Fifteen

It was an ache, being in this house. She did not have Annie. She did not have the Duke and Duchess. She didn't have her familiar maids. As much as she liked the girl that helped her here, she was unknown. And everything felt different. The bed that she slept on was new, and it reminded her of when she had first come to the Duke and Duchess of Avondale's. Reminded her of those first horrible days after the death of her father. When everything had seemed wrong. As though she had been thrust into a world she did not know. Being married to George was much like that. She did not understand this place. She did not understand her new role.

She was still grappling with what it had felt like to kiss him. Kissing.

The thought of it made her throb even now, and she threw her bedclothes off, trying desperately to find a disconnect between herself and her body.

But that was what she needed. To forget it. She had lived eighteen years never knowing what a kiss could do to one's being. Why could she not simply unknow it? Why could she not simply forget the reality of it? It would be a logical thing. A reasonable thing.

She took a breath and looked out the window. She had a view of the small garden below.

It was a rather lovely garden, for being here in the city.

Without thinking, she found herself walking out of the bedroom and down the hall wearing nothing but her night rail as she sneaked down the stairs, and out the back door that led to that garden.

It was cold out, the sky was clear and full of more stars than she had ever seen in London.

She had begun to despair of the sky here. But right now, in this waking hour, it did seem brighter, even if it could not match the country home that she loved so much. It was nights like these that made her feel connected to herself. As she had done out on the terrace.

When she had met George there.

Why did he feel inevitable? Why was it always George?

And now here she was, his wife. She could not quite piece together all of these things. She could not quite understand them. And yet, they were. Kitty walked down the path, looking at the small fruit trees that she was certain had been planted only recently. There was one tree, right at the centre, that had years to it. And she remembered what it was like to be a child. How she had climbed trees and ridden horses as if nothing could touch her.

Before she had lost her father and she had realised

that grief could touch a person more than once. That the world was unfair and frightening, and you were not taken care of.

She had thought...she had thought that losing her mother meant she might be insulated from further injury. But she had not been. And then she had come here, and the world had been a stranger. And now she found herself married to a man who was nothing like what she had thought, even when she could stand the idea of marriage.

She had not thought she would marry a stranger. She had not thought that she would marry a man who possessed the sort of beauty that could stop others in their tracks. But shared none of what Kitty valued so dearly.

Her mouth tingled when she thought of his beauty, though, and she felt... How could she feel that way? How could he have aroused this strange thing inside of her? How could it be disconnected from affection? She had always seen kissing to be simply that. A gesture of affection, and yet George had shown her it was an activity unto itself, like riding a horse. That you might thrill at it simply because you were doing it. And not because of who your mount was. So to speak.

With a restless heat boiling in her blood, she scampered to the tree at the centre and began to climb, as though she was a girl again. As though things were simple. As though they made sense.

She found herself in the top branches, a view over the wall, of the empty street, and then, she saw George. Standing out there beneath the gas lamp. What was he doing there?

He turned, as if he sensed her eyes on him, and she was smart enough to know there was no avoiding detection.

His eyes met hers. He was dressed in a black coat and hat, black gloves. His eyes glittered at her from beneath that gas lamp.

And he did not look like the George Claremont of the ballroom.

She remembered that expression he'd had the night that he had ruined her. The night he had intended to propose to Helene Parks.

He looked more like that man, and yet there was something even sharper about his appearance now. Something…something that felt vaguely like danger. She remembered that she had characterised herself as a rabbit caught in the sights of a fox one night when he had approached her. And she felt every inch that now.

At least you're safely up a tree.

George disappeared, and she knew that he had gone inside. She thought about scrambling quickly down, but he had already seen her. So what was the point of that?

She steeled herself, and she was correct in her guess that he had been heading to her. The door to the garden opened, and out walked George.

'Is the Kitty stuck in the tree?' he asked, his voice low, sardonic. And here was the George of the ballroom.

'I am not stuck,' she said.

He walked slowly down to the base of the tree and looked up. 'And what exactly are you doing, Kitty?'

'I am…I am remembering. The country. I don't like it here. I don't like London.'

'I think you made that fairly plain to everyone.'

'Isn't there anything you feel like that about? As though you want to go back? As though you want to capture something different?'

She didn't know why she was bothering to open herself up and share in this manner. She was not certain that he deserved it. But she was in a habit of sharing whatever came in her mind, and this moment was no different. He had asked, and she had answered, simply because she had not seen a purpose to hiding the truth from him. And now felt exposed, and not simply because she was in her night rail.

'Yes,' he said after a fashion. 'I think I understand that.'

'Where were you, George?'

He looked away from her. 'I had some business to see to.'

'And you cannot share what business it was with your wife?'

His mistress, likely.

The word whispered along her skin. *Mistress.* She felt as if she had a clearer understanding of what that might mean. She returned to that heated kiss in the carriage, the kiss that had involved his tongue, his teeth. It made her feel hot. Somewhat ill. The pit of her stomach was hollowed out, the place between her legs tingling, and it wounded her, to think of him in another woman's embrace, and she could not say why. Their kiss had been nothing more than a demonstration for him.

But it had been a first for her. Perhaps that was why. The way that he was able to be so dispassionate while she…

Except she recalled the way he had put her hand on him. She swallowed hard and clung yet more tightly to the tree branches.

'Are you going to stay up there all evening?'

'And if I do?' she called back.

'I shall have to come and fetch you.'

'Why?'

'I don't know. Perhaps because this is one of the things that I recall from childhood. As you just asked.'

And just like that, George Claremont began to climb the tree, as absurdly in his beautiful clothes as it was absurd for her to be in her night rail. And then, he was just one branch below her, but standing so that his face was near even with hers. 'Are you all right?'

He smelled of cheroot and whisky. And she found she could not hate the scent of it on him. She sniffed to see if she could catch a hint of perfume, but she did not, and that made her feel just slightly better. She could not quite guess at why.

'I'm all right. I'm simply…I am simply attempting to find myself in this new existence.'

He chuckled. 'Ah. I see. Is it so odd to admit that I might just understand what you mean?'

His voice was like the rest of him. Too rough and too hot. And it made her feel the same. Even knowing he'd likely been with another woman.

What was this feeling in her? White hot and burning.

'You don't know what to do with me? Because it seems as if your solution has simply been to tuck me away among your other items. And I do not create much of a bother for you.'

'Do you know, there was a time in my life when I thought my father to be a hero. The Duke of Warminster. Such a dashing figure. Everyone respected him. There were so many men who had vile reputations. Drunkards, womanisers. Men who had their estates in great debt. But not my father. No. My father managed the duchy like an insightful businessman. And yet, never strayed close to being a man of labour, lest you forget, he is a duke, and has never worked a day in his life. But he is the lord and master of all he surveys. A man above reproach. Sometimes I wish I could feel that again. It is a simplistic thing, viewing your father as a hero. But it makes the world feel quite like it has an order to it. Especially when there is succession such as ours. You think…I will be that man. I will take his place when he's gone, and I could think of nothing sadder than losing my father, but feel a sense of peace knowing that I would be the Duke of Warminster, and in that sense, all that he was would carry on. But that was before. That was before I knew who he really was.'

'And who is that?'

'A liar,' he said. 'I myself am a liar, Kitty, make no mistake. But I am honest with it.'

'So tell me a lie about where you were tonight.'

He shook his head. 'Lies don't become us, darling. We've no need for them.'

'You would simply let me wonder?'

He leaned in and she did smell whisky. Excess. And it made her hurt. 'I think you know already.'

She felt sick with it.

'Your father hurt you, and that has made you wish to simply...'

'I will not pretend. I would never seek to disappoint someone in that manner.'

'I can understand that. I suppose.'

He tilted his head then. 'Who were you, Kitty, before you came here? Because I have seen a nervous creature, who seems nearly afraid to be approached, and yet when she is, she is a hissing, spitting...a cat, I suppose. You seem fearful, and yet...you are not.'

It wasn't fair of him to ask questions about her. Not when he wouldn't answer them himself. And yet...

He compelled her.

His presence. His scent.

All of him.

'It is not fear. It is...that I do not understand. And that creates a level of... It makes me wish to stay out of the centre of everything. That is for the best, because look where being at the centre got me.'

'But you climbed trees when you were a girl?'

She banished the weight in her chest brought on by George's certain admission that he had been with another woman. 'I climbed trees. And rode horses. My opinions were welcome. My father liked to talk about the world with me. And how we might run it better. He married a maid, you know.'

'Yes, I do. Because it was quite the scandal, and I am old enough to remember it.'

'Well. He did not see why the world had to run in such a fashion that his marriage would create a stir. That he should have to flee to the country to live a life. We talked about those things. He did not shy away from them.'

'In that regard, I think your father respected your intelligence more than mine ever has.'

'It is strange, to live among people who seem so happy to maintain the illusion of a society that benefits so few. My father did not accept such things. And he did not teach me to.'

'Poor Kitty. And then you moved to London, where you discovered that your opinions, as a woman, would never be valued.'

'Yes. I did. It has been a lowering experience.'

'For that I do apologise. For I do not wish to see you lowered.'

'You don't?'

'No.' The word was like silk on her skin. 'I rather enjoy your tirades. Most especially I enjoy watching people have to contend with them.'

'Even when I unleash them upon you?'

'Almost most especially. It makes for a thrilling evening. Especially when one has been quite bored up until that point.'

'Well, I'm glad to know that I can occasionally inject some interest into the day.'

'You do quite.'

'George,' she said. 'Do you not ever think…do you not ever think of what you could change?'

He paused for a moment, and in the moonlight, just then, with his eyes dark and bleak, and his expression like marble, Kitty was breathless. George was beautiful. And that was all she could think. He was… He made her ache. He was brilliant, and funny. And quite simply the most beautiful man she had ever seen. And he was concerned with nothing but his own pleasure, it would seem. He was hers, and yet he never could be.

And just then, it made her heart feel as though it was being split apart. She had no idea what this feeling was. This desperate need to hold tight to another person. Was this simply grief? An echo of it left over from the loss of her father? Something that made her feel as if she desperately needed to hang on to another person? For she had been ripped away from certainty yet again and placed into something unknown. And George was tall and strong and capable, and perhaps that was why she wished to grab hold of his shoulders and steady herself with them.

What she really wanted to do was grab those shoulders and shake him. Ask for him to be what she wanted him to be. Ask for him to feel the same things that she did. The same convictions. The same…depth.

'When I was a boy, I thought that the world was the duchy. The town house that we lived in when we went to London. Eton. When I was a boy, I thought I knew every piece of the world. And I was certain of my father's ability to control it. We were safe and fed and loved. My sister Dorothea…she was such a wonderful child. Beautiful and best beloved. I felt as if the world were a rather charmed place. I had a dog. A hunting dog. He was the most beautiful thing you'd ever seen. He got into a fight with a fox. Diseased, my father speculated. And it caused concern. I asked my father, I begged him, to fix the situation. For I was certain that the Duke of Warminster could fix anything. He went away for a while and came back, and he told me it was fixed. The next day, I was given a new puppy. But my dog was gone. My father told me he had shot her. He said it was the only thing that could've been done.'

'Oh, George,' she said, feeling a deep well of sympathy in her heart.

'It was the first time I understood that for my father, fixing something might mean something different than what I believed. I had thought it meant setting things to rights. But in his mind, it meant preserving our lives by ending another. I'm not so foolish as to believe it might not have been necessary. I'm a grown man. Animals with such diseases can harm humans. And will eventually die themselves. I'm not calling my father a monster for that action. I'm simply saying it was…informative. Instructive.'

'I am still sorry.'

'You lost your father, Kitty, I am not comparing our losses. But…no, I have never wished to fix the world the way my father does.'

'But in your own way?'

'I have made my own way,' he said.

'Have you ever loved anyone?' Did he love his mistress? She wanted to know. Even if the answer were yes. Kitty did not know what she thought of love. But she wanted to know what George thought, because she was married to him. Because she wanted to know him. Something. Anything.

'No,' he said. 'I have to say, I find that within the bounds of the aristocracy love is not a recognised concept. There is duty, and there is…a selective affection applied to those they deem worthy of it. The love that I've experienced has been outside the bonds of society.'

'Like my father?' Of course, his mistress was rumoured to be a ballerina, and so she wouldn't be part of polite society. It made sense, what he said.

'In a fashion, maybe. I'm not a romantic, though. I'm a realist. Whatever people think about me. I simply don't deny what I am. They play games, and they manipulate. I play games with them.'

'And will you play such games with me?'

She looked down at him, and he looked up at her for a long moment. He climbed up another tree branch, changing their positions, making it so he was looking down at her, which she was much more accustomed to. 'I will do my level best not to play games with you. If you were one of those silly girls caught up in these debutante games…perhaps, I would find a game worth playing. But there is something in you that's real, Kitty. I should not like to damage that. The world has done quite enough to you as it is.'

She looked at him, and she tried to see George as she had seen him that day at the egg-shaped ball. Holding her yarn and looking at her sardonically. But that image was mixed now with the man who had kissed her. The one who had just told her about the loss of his dog. The one who spoke of his disillusionment both with the world and his father in flat, stoic tones that made her feel broken. The man who had been out tonight doing things that were still a mystery to her. The man she was married to. All the different pieces of George. They were fractured, and it made her heart feel as if it were too. And she was not…accustomed to this. To having a care for her own comfort. Her own feelings. And yet she felt consumed with it now.

She wanted to touch him. And she…she found herself reaching her hand up to his face. She traced the line of his jaw, and he closed his eyes as if he were a beast that she was soothing.

'George,' she whispered. And she could not explain the strange sensations that rioted through her. Could not explain what compelled her then.

Except that he was beautiful. And he broke her heart.

So many times, that had been said to her. A handsome man. That was a desirable quality in a husband. She had not understood why. But part of her thought that whatever happened in her marriage, if she could spend the rest of for ever looking at his face…

It might sustain her.

And it might shatter her.

It might do both.

This felt like a new dimension of grief. But there was a sweetness to the bitterness, and she could not put words to it. So she touched his face. Felt that crisp stubble beneath her fingertips. Moved her fingertips to his chin, pressing her thumb there at the cleft of it. His lips curved upward slightly. And he opened his eyes, taking hold of her wrist and moving her hand away. 'Easy,' he said.

'What?'

'You mustn't toy with me.'

'I'm not,' she said.

The look in his eyes became grave. 'I believe that. Because you've never said anything untrue in your life, have you?'

'I wouldn't know how.'

'Oh, Kitty. You must be careful with that. There are those who would seek to break this part of you.'

'Who can? Who could get close enough? I'm your wife now.'

He nodded, his expression grim. 'So you are. I wish that meant you were safer.'

She shivered.

'You're cold,' he said. 'Let's go inside.'

He began to climb down the tree, and she followed. He reached the ground first, and when she was near to the last branch, he reached up and gripped her waist, and lifted her down as if she weighed nothing.

His hands were warm, and just so very large...

His thumb skimmed her ribcage, and it sent a spark along her body that ignited into a river of fire that seemed to flow through her bloodstream with alarming speed. And she knew now, from before, that her breasts would get heavy, and the space between her legs would begin to feel right. The place that she often ignored, and it would become insistent. And it did.

She looked up at him, feeling desperate for answers.

'Do not ask me such questions,' he said.

'I didn't speak.'

'You do not know what you asked,' he said, his tone indulgent. 'And that is the danger. Because I do know. And I know how to answer each and every question, but I fear, that I should shock you.'

And she thought of where he had been.

She nodded slowly and stepped away from him, extricated herself from his hold. Because she wanted him to answer those questions, but not freshly returned from an evening with someone else. She might be innocent of the ways of things between men and women, but she knew enough to know that she did not want his mouth on hers so soon after it had been on another woman's. She might not know how these things work, but she knew herself. And she was confident in that.

'Goodnight, George,' she said.

'Goodnight, Kitty.'

But when she went back inside, sleep proved elusive. And when she dreamed, it was of George. And the way it had felt for his mouth to be pressed on hers.

George cursed himself as a fool. He should not have climbed the tree after Kitty last night, but she had seen him standing out on the street. And then he had gone and made her think that he had been unfaithful to her. And watching the way her beautiful, proud face had shuddered against the force of that had been... She cared. She cared whether or not he was unfaithful.

Hell, he cared too.

He would take her as his wife soon enough, but he felt...on edge. She was an innocent.

He did not want her to be afraid when he took her to bed. He did not wish...

It is the ferocity of what you feel for her that holds you back, and you well know it. You bloody coward.

He did not like it. When he had kissed her in the

carriage on their wedding day, it had been an attempt at seizing control.

And yet he had not found it. Not then.

Instead, he had found himself caught up in her. In his need for her.

He could not touch her. Not as he was.

He felt… He did not feel as if he could trust himself.

And yet she pushed him. To the brink, and she had no idea. He wished to part her legs and feast upon her. That desire that had seized him in the study had not been for Helene. He knew that. For it was the touch of his hand to her thigh that had ignited his need.

And that had been Kitty. Purely Kitty.

He had had any number of lovers, all experienced, and all immaterial.

Kitty was not immaterial. She was his wife.

And last night when he'd spoken to her he'd felt so close to being understood. It was the damnedest thing, and at the same time he'd known…

He could not tell her his true aim. If anyone found out what he was about, everyone in his life would be in danger.

And Kitty…

Kitty spoke from her heart. With conviction at all times. She could get herself killed if she knew too much.

When she appeared in the doorway of his study at half past ten in the morning, looking as if she had not slept at all, his body went tight.

'Good morning.'

'Yes. Good morning. I had thought to ask…do you have a library?'

'Yes.'

'May I make use of it?'

'Of course.'

He thought of the books that he had there. Abolitionist texts and other political works. She would be surprised, considering. But she would also find many hours of enjoyment in it, he knew.

And he found he wanted to give her something, since he had to hide so much away. A peek into himself by letting her see the library. She had made him feel as if all he had done was take from her, which would be funny, if he did not feel so much as though it were true. For he was far above her in rank, and it was a good match for her. He should feel as though he had done nothing but elevate her. But he did not.

'I'll show you.'

'Oh, no. I simply wanted your permission.'

'You wanted my permission?'

She lifted a shoulder. 'It seemed polite.'

'Come on,' he said.

Her dark hair was up today, a few delicate ringlets framing her face. She was wearing a gown of deep purple, and he could not help but admire the way the darker colour complemented her.

He opened the door to the room, which had wall-to-wall books, and watched as her eyes lit with wonder. 'In the absence of large fields in which to ride horses, I will take a good book.'

'You can always climb the tree again.'

She looked at him, and her cheeks went pink. She felt it. This thing between them.

He thought of how she'd looked last night. That gown made her look like an angel. But he of course had wanted to try to see if he could catch sight of her dusky nipples through the thin fabric. It had been too dark to do so.

She looked as if she wanted to speak, but could not make words form. Her throat worked, her lips pursing.

'I should like… Do you have anything on the history of London? I feel as if I want to know more. Rather than simply… I want to understand what people find beautiful here?' There was something desperate in it. Her need to understand. And he knew that it was about more than simply London.

And suddenly, she stretched up on her toes, and pressed her mouth to his. He wrapped his arm around her waist and simply held her as she kissed him. He did not take the lead. He allowed her to do it. The kiss was breathless, and her lips were closed, but he could feel an immense amount of need behind it. Not desire, as much as a desperate urge to understand what marriage was. To understand what they were.

He did not know the answer any more than she did. He only knew what made her heart beat faster, and what made her want to draw closer to him. It was not anything half so sweet as care or love, as she might hope. It was lust. He desperately lusted after this woman. His bride.

'George,' she whispered, pulling away from him, her eyes glittering. 'I…'

He traced a line down her cheek. 'Yes?'

'What is this?'

'You want me to possess you,' he said, the words coming out hard. 'You want me to strip you naked, and taste every inch of you.'

'How is that possible?'

'Because you desire me.'

'Do you desire me?'

'Remember what I showed you in the carriage?'

'Oh.'

'I would happily lift your skirts and sink my cock into you now.' She swallowed hard, her eyes widened, a bit wild. 'But what I should like, Kitty, is for it to be undeniable for you. I would take you, as an animal. I could take your virgin body and make you mine, make you cry out with it. But are you ready?'

She shook her head. 'No.'

'I didn't think so.'

He ignored the stab of disappointment in his gut. 'These books here are about London,' he said, pointing to a section on one shelf. 'You may read them.'

And then he turned and left the library as quickly as possible.

Chapter Sixteen

When Kitty woke up the following morning, in an unfamiliar bed, in an unfamiliar room, she still could scarcely believe that she was married. She did not feel changed. Rather, the only thing that felt different at all was the environment around her.

George had left her to be by herself again last night. And this could not be the marriage bed, because she was given to understand that what would happen between them would take place in a shared bed.

She couldn't imagine sharing a bed with him.

She remembered climbing the tree.

She remembered what he'd said to her in the library yesterday morning. Hot, rough offers that had done something to her soul.

She remembered the kiss.

It had been wild. It made her heart gallop like a frightened horse even now to think about it.

She lay there, the bedclothes pulled up just under her chin, and she tried to recapture that moment in her mind.

But none of the notes that she made for herself to

refer back to could capture it. It had been warm and comforting, but disconcerting all at once. The slide of his tongue against hers the most incandescent and unexpected pleasure of her life. And if any one thing could have made her begin to understand the words that he had spoken to her, it was that.

Tell him to make it pleasurable. Rather than fast.

She had not understood the concept of pleasure between two people in quite that way. She had always seen kissing as a gesture of affection. Much like a hug. A gesture typically reserved for those with a romantic connection, but she had not thought...

She did not know that there was a more intimate expression of it. And that it made your body feel as if a small fire had been started in your stomach, one that burns down shamefully between your legs.

Maybe it was simply a London thing. Maybe it was not done in the country.

She laughed at the absurdity of that thought. That truly did come from naivety, and she could admit it, even if only to herself here in the quiet of the bedchamber. Because of course, if people knew that you could do that, they would all do it. And perhaps that was the real reason why you weren't allowed to be alone on terraces—or anywhere else with men. The people who knew about this would certainly be taken with it. Obsessed with it. Keen to try again at any opportunity.

Except...unexpectedly, it was as if the kiss had altered her in two different ways. It had injected into her a sense of understanding that had not been there before. Not wholly. Something that made sense of the hand beneath her dress and the way it had felt. The way it had been to stand with him on that moonlit terrace. The way she was fascinated with how he smoked the cheroot, even while she found it vile.

Yes, it had made sense of some of those things, but also, it had pushed a sliver of doubt beneath her skin, one that seemed to carry a poison that was spreading. She felt…uncertain and caring of what her husband thought of her.

Her husband.

Perhaps it was simply that he was her husband, and no longer Lord Curran, a near stranger that she did not know, and should barely give a second thought to.

She did not understand the true purpose of marriage. Her father had loved her mother, and he had changed his entire life to be with her. They'd had her, and her mother had died a scant two years later giving birth to another child, who had also died. Love had been what had brought them together. Not anything else. They had not been suitable to one another, they had not enriched one another's purses. Her father had been desperately hurt when he had lost her mother.

She had never known her mother, not really, not beyond vague memories and impressions, and she had seen only the ghost of their relationship throughout her growing up years. And then here, in London, it was all about what the marriage could get you. All about what it could make you. All about the business of joining. Titles, finances, and everything else. But business it was.

She got the impression that the Duke and Duchess of Avondale had something different between them than that. And suddenly, she wanted to ask George. What did he expect?

He had not come to her bed last night. And that… that pushed the poison deeper into her veins. That made her question everything.

She got out of bed, and saw that a fire had already been lit, which meant the maids had already been in. She began to look around the room, wondering if she would be dressing herself this morning, which was fine—she dressed herself in the country—it was only that the clothing they wore in London was a bit more complicated, but nothing she could not master.

A moment later, the door opened, and in came a girl she had never seen before.

'Good morning, Lady Curran,' she said.

The title brought Kitty up short. A few days with it had not made it familiar.

'Good morning.'

'The Marquess has hired me to be your lady's maid.'

'Oh.'

'The other maids said that you were beautiful. It's true.'

The girl was beaming, as if she had just won a fortune. She was quite young, something that startled Kitty slightly, as typically someone who had achieved the position of lady's maid had a bit of experience.

'What are you called?'

'Lizzie,' the girl said. 'Thank you for asking.'

'Of course.'

'I heard that you had many new, beautiful dresses here.' She opened a large armoire in the corner to reveal a suite of clothing that Kitty had never seen before.

'Beautiful,' the girl said.

Kitty felt hot all over. A whole suite of new clothing. It was the very thing she was worried about. The very thing that consumed her. Clothing. Fabrics. Cotton.

She said nothing as the girl took a gloriously beautiful butter-yellow gown from the armoire and began to help her dress. She would have to speak to George. Of course, the clothing was made and purchased, but… it could not happen again. Her old things needed to be brought from the Duke and Duchess's house. She had not asked for anything new, and while she knew that a trousseau was common when one was married, while she knew that a married lady would be expected to dress differently than a debutante…

Was she even a married lady? They had spoken vows, but they had not gone to the marriage bed. She was given to understand that was important.

'And where is the Marquess this morning?'

'His study, I believe,' the girl said, as she began to fuss with Kitty's hair.

'Thank you.' She looked at her reflection. And for the first time in her memory, she found herself wondering what someone else might see if they were to look at her. Her dark hair spilled from its style, falling around her shoulders, little crystal stars placed in her curls to great effect. Her eyes looked wide and frightened, and this particular colour yellow made her complexion look just a bit fragile.

She did not like it, because it was a reflection of what she felt.

Fragile and delicate and on the verge of breaking.

She had never before felt the need to hide herself. Not beyond the physical sense, of course. But she had never felt the driving need to conceal something deeper. And just now she did. She very well did.

She tried to find some strength. Something. She imagined her little country house, she imagined herself there. And she remembered who she was. She might've been tossed around by society, by the winds of fate and of life, but she was still Kitty Fitzroy. It did not matter what title she was given. She was her father's daughter. He was a man who had abandoned propriety for passion. He was a man who lived a life he believed in. She would not forget. Not ever.

She steeled herself and bid her lady's maid farewell as she walked out of her bedchamber and stood there in the wholly unfamiliar house. She had been outside of herself when she had arrived the day before yesterday. She truly had not seen the place. It was beautiful. Sedate in a way she had not imagined George's home might be. There were no frescoes of nude Roman goddesses, which, frankly, had been her expectation.

She went down the stairs, and paused. She needed directions, she realised. She was a bit foolish. Going about the place without actually knowing the lay of it.

'Ah, my lady. I was about to have you sent for. The Marquess is in the dining room.' The housekeeper, Mrs Brown—she at least remembered that brief introduction from yesterday—smiled at her warmly, and it made her want to weep. 'Breakfast is ready.'

He was waiting for her? She had imagined that she

was going to have to beard the lion in his den so to speak. But apparently he was prepared to see her.

She walked in and was shocked. Both by the glorious spread of food, and the sight of her husband sitting down at the far end of the table. He looked as though he had not slept at all the previous night. He looked more debauched than she had ever seen him. She wondered where he had been the previous night.

For it had not been in her bed. That much was certain.

Unless he had tossed and turned beneath the bedclothes the entire night, he had to have been elsewhere.

'Good morning,' he said, his voice rough. He sounded as though he thought it was anything but a good morning at all.

'I need to speak with you,' she said, not changing her direction, even though she had not—as expected—had to seek him out, but had instead been summoned to the dining room at his behest.

'Yes?' He lifted a brow.

'You had an entire new wardrobe procured for me without speaking to me.'

'Is it not to your liking?'

'I can only assume that you mean in terms of fashion. I have opposition to the way the fabric is being produced.'

'I did not get you a factory-made garment.'

'You…you didn't?'

'I paid quite handsomely for textiles done by hand. And I can verify that the source of the material was not slave labour.'

'Really?'

'Yes.'

'Such things exist?'

'If you are willing to look for them. And pay for them. You will find that many are not.'

'Oh.'

She tried to look at him, really look at him, because suddenly, in her estimation, the entirety of all that he was had shifted. She felt as if she knew nothing, least of all anything about him. And given the way that her world was still utterly and completely altered from the fact that she was married at all…it was a bit much.

'You care about such things?'

'You do. And you have never been quiet about it. I would have to be dead or uncaring to ignore it. Though it might pain you to know this, I am neither.'

'No. I suppose you aren't.'

'Have a seat.'

'Were you out last night?' she asked. She sat three chairs away from him and took a piece of toasted bread from the plate.

'Yes. I saw no reason to change my usual habits.'

'I see.'

She did not know why she found that to be sad.

'Did you find ways to amuse yourself?'

'Truthfully, I fell asleep immediately. Yesterday was difficult.'

'Yes. I know it is very difficult to make for yourself an excellent match and take yourself off the marriage market.'

'You're angry with me,' she said.

'I'm not angry with you. What happened was not your fault. You were quite literally asleep.'

'I cannot decide if that's worse or better. That you hold me blameless is one thing, but the truth is, then you see me as simply a hapless victim of all of this, and that makes you still the most important piece of all of this, doesn't it?'

'I can't say as I considered it in those terms.'

Here she was in this man's house—in her house—and yet she had no more power than she'd had a week ago. This would be it. Everything there was. If she said nothing. If she pushed for nothing.

'Well, I have. Because I am eternally and chronically unimportant. The thing that is moved around whenever fate or one of the men in my life deems it suitable. I have no control over anything.'

'You are now a married woman. Take responsibility for the household. Take some responsibility for what you might build.'

'With what?'

'Pardon me?' He paused with his cup of coffee held halfway towards his mouth.

'With what shall I make these changes? Do you have plans? A specific allowance that your father is giving you to give to me?'

He laughed. 'I do not need funds from my father. I can manage on my own, thank you.'

'That does not seem to be the common thought on your position.'

'No. Indeed. But I find I am unconcerned with common thought.'

'Well. We both know that isn't true. You were quite happy to compete for the title of society's most scandalous. Though I suppose now that you have hastily married you cannot claim that.'

'I don't suppose.' He looked at her. 'I was planning on marrying anyway.'

'I know,' she said. Would he have taken Helene Parks to the marriage bed on their wedding night? She did wonder. And more, she wondered about the specifics of the marriage bed.

She would not ask again, though. It made her feel foolish. She was tired of that. The same as she was tired of feeling like an object of least concern in all of this. Oh, her reputation might be paramount, but no one truly cared about the state of her happiness.

'So you see, this changes nothing for me.'

'Again, how fortunate. For it changes everything for me.'

'No, Kitty. It changes nothing.'

He was right, and that hurt worse. Nothing had changed. She was an attachment he had not asked for, as she had been for her aunt and uncle. She was nothing more.

'And if anything has changed,' he continued, 'it is your good fortune. You might not have been accepting of the fact that you needed to marry, but you did. There is no other way for you. No other way for me. Here we are with each other.'

'Yes. Here we are.'

And suddenly, she found her chest crowded with concerns. What she might do to be useful, yes, but others as well. How was she to make a life with this man, and what did that even look like?

'What is it you want from a wife?'

'I need a wife who will see to the running of the household.'

He said that as if it was a well-practised answer.

'But your staff sees to the running of the household.'

'But now planning menus and that sort of thing will fall to you.'

'Not to the cook?'

'Well, she will continue to oversee. As she does. But…you will see to the running of the household, you will fulfil your position as my wife.'

'You mean, in the sense that a marquess needs a marchioness, and a duke will need a duchess?'

'Yes. Precisely in that sense.'

'Because you will need children.'

'Yes.'

'So we are to have children together.'

'Yes,' he said. 'That is how it works.'

'And will you take your place in the House of Lords? Will you become politically active?'

'That is how it works,' he said again, his voice dead-pan.

'Why haven't you done it yet? Why have you taken no interest in anything before?'

'It is very difficult to take up political seats when one is in his cups every night and hung over every morning.'

He said it with an air of humour. She did not know what to make of it.

'And yet, you just showed me that you know how to

procure items that have caused minimal harm to the world. Which means you actually have a great many more thoughts in your head than you pretend to have. And I… The man that I spoke to that night out on the terrace…he was much more thoughtful than any other version of you that I have encountered.'

'Then one would be forced to conclude that he is an apparition, don't you think?' With a flick of his wrist, he salted his poached egg. It was done elegantly and somehow insistently, and she had no idea how he managed both.

She felt so conscious then of a pane of glass being erected between them. And she could press her palms against it, press her face against it, and it would still not give her a clear vision of the man behind it. It was as if everything he said to her was muffled. Yes, she could understand it, but she was certain there was more beneath it, and she could not understand why exactly that was.

'When will I meet your family?'

'We will not be able to avoid it for ever,' he said. 'Unfortunately.'

'You do not get along with them?'

'No,' he said.

'You told me…you told me that your father was not who you believed him to be.'

He sighed heavily. 'What do you know of the Claremont family?'

'That it is an old family, and there have been no scandals associated with the name before Dorothea and Freddie eloped…'

'A feat accomplished by keeping those around you afraid of you, rather than exemplary behaviour. And therein lies a rather serious issue, I find.'

'What exactly are you saying?'

'My father had a bastard child,' he said. 'In truth, I believe my father has more than one bastard child.'

She flinched. 'Oh. I am given to understand that is quite common among the aristocracy.'

'Yes. It would be expected with someone like me. It is not expected with someone like my father.'

'Do you…?'

'I do not.'

'How can you be certain?'

'I am certain.'

He eyed her speculatively. But he did not say what he was thinking. And so, she decided to ask the question herself, to spare them both.

'You say that what is done for procreation is also done for…recreation.'

He laughed. And it surprised her because it seemed genuine. And she felt a small, answering smile tug at the corner of her mouth, even while she felt she should maybe be indignant.

He was, after all, making fun of her by laughing. Except it did not feel that way. It felt a good deal more friendly.

'Yes. That is a very good way of putting it.'

'And it is kissing but more. It is… You said in the library that you would possess me.'

'Kitty,' he said, his voice a warning.

'We're married,' she said.

'Kitty, I do not understand you. You ran from me yesterday. Yet you push me here?'

'Well, I had expected that when I married, I would feel different. And instead, everything around me changed, and a different person dictates all that I do, and yet nothing of the world feels new to me. Or more. I don't feel as if I've discovered anything.'

Kitty knew why she had told him no. Because the things he had made her feel were overwhelming. Because they made her feel terrified. Because she was not used to being overtaken by the needs of her own body. And it felt at odds with what she had attempted to fashion herself into. But now…now, she wanted more. Now, she wanted everything. She was ready now. She had accepted it. This desire. It was part of her.

And she…she wanted. She wanted more than simply for the world to be an easier place. She wanted him. She wanted George Claremont. Whoever he was. She wanted George Claremont, even if she could not understand him. She was passionately, desperately desirous of his hands on her body, of the possession that he had spoken of in the library.

And she wanted to find her way back to that. To push him to that moment again. She wanted…

She just wanted.

'I did not wish to push you into anything.'

'Of course.'

'Tell me this, Kitty, what is it you expect from a husband?'

'I was not aware that I was permitted to have expectations.'

'Since when do you care what you are permitted to do or not do?'

'What I mean to say is, I was unaware a woman was able to have any say in anything beyond the initial selection. It was my understanding that you had better be unerring in that initial choice, for you would suffer from it for ever if you chose wrong.'

'Who would you have chosen, then? Not Lord Boredom.'

She recoiled. 'No. But I had thought of a man who might die quickly. And leave me a widow. It seemed not a terrible idea.'

'Indeed it is not,' he said. 'It would certainly afford a woman more freedom.'

'That was my thought.'

'A good thought, Kitty. Quite a good thought.'

She could not tell if he was making fun of her or not.

'And so you had no designs on marrying for love or for passion.'

'No.'

'And yet, you resisted marrying me. Why exactly?'

'Because I felt strongly that we would not suit. We don't know anything about each other.'

'Do we not?'

She thought about that for a long moment. 'Perhaps we do not like anything about each other.'

Except she had liked the way he kissed. And she had liked the way he had spoken to her out on that terrace. And even now, she could not quite hate the way that he spoke to her. She liked to watch his hands as he did mundane things like eat his breakfast. And she wished very much that she could explain to herself why that was.

And as suddenly as he had salted the egg, he was up out of his seat, and he reached out and pulled her up from hers.

And with no warning whatsoever, he dropped his head, and kissed her.

Chapter Seventeen

It was like a fire, all-consuming, and he should not have done it. He was far too affected by last night. He had sabotaged the factory. It was not complete enough but he would not risk setting fire to the place, not when it could destroy everything around it.

He still had Stanton's factories to go after, but this was one of the best courses of action he could've taken, and he'd done it. Still, the enormity of it, of the work that needed to be done in the aftermath… He still felt no closer to fixing anything. Certainly no closer to avenging Hannah. And here was his wife. His wife. Was he not entitled to kiss her? In truth, he had not been with a woman in a very long time, and while all of the *ton* might believe him to be constantly in various women's beds, there had been no time. He could not attend to a London Season, attempt to dismantle the evils of society, and take his pleasure.

But she had smiled. Just very small. And only just at the edges of her mouth, but she had done it. And it had ignited something inside of him. Along with her openness, that innocence. That beguiling curiosity that begged him to teach her what he knew.

And it made him feel the worst sort of rake, but she was his wife. She was his wife, dammit. And could he not slake his lust with his wife?

She whimpered, and he cupped the back of her head, taking the kiss deeper. She had never been kissed. That much had been apparent the day before yesterday in the carriage. She had not been kissed, and she was hungry. Because what he knew about Kitty Claremont—for she was a Claremont now—was that she had an unquenchable passion lurking beneath her breast, and while she might not know of all the delectable ways that she could unleash that passion, he did. He knew what it was to burn the way that she did. Truly. But it was not only injustice that could light a fire between them.

It was this.

And so he kissed her. Letting his tongue go deep, and when she gasped, deeper still. He licked her, tasting her. She was like coffee and sweet jam, and he couldn't get enough of her.

It was the question there in that kiss. The innocence in it.

And he felt like the worst sort of cad for glorying in it, but glory he did.

He licked her upper lip, her lower lip, nipped her, and made her gasp. And he did not regret it.

She was right now everything he needed, and if someone would've told him that Kitty would contain all he needed he would've called them a fool.

But there was something about knowing she cared that made this all the sweeter. That his gesture with the wardrobe had been met initially with fury, because where the material came from meant something to her. It was that common spark, that was what intrigued him. That was what spurred him on. That was what made him want to take her. Endlessly. Gloriously. He moved both hands to hold her face as he continued to kiss her. And he felt her petite body trembling in his hold.

'I'll show you,' he said, his words a growl. 'I'll show you what transpires between a man and wife.'

'More?'

'Yes,' he growled. 'I will show you. But you must tell me if I frighten you.'

'Why would I be frightened?' she asked, her teeth chattering.

'Because it is unknown. Because it may hurt. At first.'

Her eyes went round. 'Will it?'

That had not occurred to her.

It was clear by the expression on her face. But what did she know? He had spoken to her in euphemism. He had not been particularly helpful. But he had known that if he spoke of anatomy, and if he had spoken of how things were in absolutely blunt terms, he only would have frightened her.

And he would've aroused himself. Therein lay the issue with the gulf between them.

'I have never lain with a virgin,' he confessed, because he thought perhaps confessing his own inexperience on that score might make things even, though he could also see how she might have wanted him to have a prior understanding of what to do with a virgin's body. But it was no matter. He knew how to arouse a woman.

He would arouse her.

'Does that matter?'

'Yes, darling. It does. You will see. You will understand.'

And then it was as if she was racing towards it. She closed the distance between them, kissing him, and this time, directing things. As if she was in a hurry to get to that point.

'What is it?' he asked, looking at her.

'I am tired of being told that I will understand soon. I want to understand now. Everything. So much of this world makes no sense to me, and if I am standing at the threshold of understanding any one new thing, then I will take hold of it. I will race through.'

'Remember. Pleasurable. Not fast.'

The admonishment made her cheeks colour, and he wondered if she even understood why.

But it was the most beautiful thing he had ever seen. Right up there with the faint smile he had earned not long ago.

He kissed her, right there in the dining room. As if none of the staff could walk in at any moment. But what did it matter? She was his wife.

She was his.

He had precious little in this life that belonged to him.

The title was his father's, and it meant nothing to him. The minute that the aristocracy had been exposed to him for what it was, it had meant nothing. And he had been torn all of his life between wanting to burn it all to the ground, and wanting to find some way to use it to make things matter. To make change.

There were reasons that he had not joined Parliament. Why he had not got involved in politics. There were rules to politics. It was a chess game and one had to play within the bounds of it. And he was not interested in playing by rules.

He did not want to do anything that might raise suspicion about his interests, or about his actions.

He did understand where she was coming from, but it was nothing he had not considered himself many times over the years.

He felt, strongly, that he could serve the world better as he did.

Because he did what few men were willing to dare and to do. Because he knew that the consequences that he would face would be limited.

And so he could act with a certain level of impunity. But his pursuit had become all that he was, and he called not his time, and not even the ways in which he conducted himself, his own. He put on a performance for society, and a relentless battle away from it.

But this moment…this was her. And it was him.

She had intrigued him from the first, and he never would've thought that it would lead here, but it had.

And what he did not understand was the intense surge of possessiveness that roared through him. But it had been there. It had been there for a long time. Certainly before he had found her sleeping in the *chaise longue* in the study.

Certainly before he had discovered the skin on her thigh was creamy and soft, and made him wish to explore the silken space between her thighs.

His.

She was his. And he would make her want him. He would earn a smile, a real smile, and he would earn her cries of pleasure.

She knew nothing of the pleasure to be found between men and women, and he would make it his personal mission to have her know that it could be limitless.

He had never expected to enjoy the thought of so much power. That her sexual appetite could be determined by what he did tonight.

That it would be entirely his.

He preferred women who had a certain amount of knowledge when it came to the act. The things that they knew they had been taught by their previous lovers, and he was more than pleased with that. Happy to benefit from prior experience.

But not with Kitty. The way that she kissed would always be a blade honed in the fire between them. The way that she caressed a man's body would be informed by what he taught her.

He thought of everything, all the darkness of these past months. The ways that his pursuits had crashed down around him, the ways in which he had not managed to fix it all, no matter how hard he tried.

He thought of that, and he let it all fade away. Because did he not deserve this moment? This woman.

'Come.'

But he did not wait for her to follow, rather he swept

her up off her feet, and carried her from the dining room. She looked bewildered, wrapping her arms around his neck as he took her from the room and began to take them both upstairs.

'George,' she said, her voice trembling. He carried her down the hall, to his bedchamber, and he opened the door, revealing the large bed at the centre of the room.

'Do you have doubts?'

She shook her head. 'I wish to know.'

'Because you are curious, or because your body desires me?'

She looked worried, uncertain, and that was not an expression he was accustomed to seeing on Kitty's face.

'What?'

'I find myself unwilling to speak the truth, for I'm afraid that I desire you and you do not desire me. It's those feelings. The ones that you described to me on our wedding day.'

She was just so innocent. But something had to change that. He was her husband. She would have his heir.

He gritted his teeth. An heir was another thing he had tortured himself over.

But if the duchy fell into someone else's hands, they might be like his father. He would try to make his son like him.

He would try to leave behind a legacy that cared for the lives of others.

He would try to erase the pain created by the Claremont name.

And he could only do that by carrying forward this

burning conviction. And Kitty…Kitty would teach their children. That made his need for her leap all the higher.

'I desire you,' he said. 'Remember what I told you?'

He took her hand again, and pressed it to the falls of his trousers. He knew she could feel him there, hard and ready for her.

She looked skittish, but she did not pull her hand away. Instead, she cupped him, moving her fingertips slowly over his length.

'I want you. A man cannot fake that. Cannot manufacture desire such as that.'

'I had thought, that while statues are carved from marble, that the thing hanging between their legs looked fleshy.'

It was not something he expected for her to say.

'Yes, because the statues are not aroused.'

'And it changes when you're aroused?'

'Yes. Tell me, Kitty. Are you wet between your legs?'

He could see her posture change, and he imagined that she was squeezing her thighs together, trying to mitigate her physical response to his question, because while she might not fully understand what it was that was taking place between them, she did want him.

'Yes,' she whispered.

'We are in the same state. We desire one another.' He turned her around so that she was facing away from him, and began to work the ties of her gown. A short gasp escaped her lips as the top layer fell away from her body, leaving her standing there in a chemise.

He could see the delicate points of her nipples standing up against the fabric, and he let his hands span her waist, moving them up slowly, toying with the underside of her breasts, until she gasped.

'Where do you want me to touch you?'

'It's…it's curious. How parts of my body feel alive.'

'Where do you want me to touch you?'

'My… I can't say.'

'Tell me,' he said, holding her tightly, his breath flowing across her neck, and he saw her shiver from it.

'My breasts,' she said, the word a whisper.

'Here?' he asked, cupping just the rounded part of her.

'Not quite.'

'Ah,' he said, his tone knowing. He moved his hand to her nipple and pinched her. 'Here.'

'Yes,' she gasped.

'You're filled with desire, Kitty. And you might not know all the steps to the dance, but you are ready.'

'Yes,' she said. 'I'm ready.'

He moved his other hand to her breast, and he began to tease both nipples with his thumbs. They got harder still beneath his ministrations, and then he turned her to face him, dropping down to his knees. He removed her shoes. Began to let his hands move up beneath her dress. She had stockings on, and he tried to imagine what sort of ribbon might be at the top. It made him feel hungry.

Then he moved to her bare thigh, where he had touched her that night in the study. He felt her tremble beneath his touch.

'I wish to see you,' he said. 'All of you.'

He gripped the hem of the chemise and pulled it up

over her head. And she was standing there simply in the stockings, the dark thatch of curls between her thighs framed elegantly by pale skin. The sight of her slightly rounded stomach made him ache, and her small waist and palm-sized breasts were glory. Each nipple was the colour of a ripened cherry, and he found he wanted to taste them. 'You mentioned statues before. You are like what I've seen of Aphrodite,' he said.

The flush from her cheeks began to cover the rest of her skin. And so he kissed her again, because he knew that it would help her forget. He knew that it would make her think of nothing beyond how much she wanted him. Beyond how much she wanted this.

He kissed her neck, her collarbone, down to the point of her breast, where he drew her deep into his mouth, and she held his head to her while he sucked.

'I still don't understand,' she gasped. 'Who makes these rules? These rules of society, these rules of…'

'What do you mean?'

'Who decided that it would feel so good to have a man…? This seems improbable.'

'It is not a rule, and that is the beauty of this. There is no rule.' He cupped her breast and pinched her other nipple. 'There are no rules at all here. There is only want. Only desire. There is nothing but what feels good. But what feels right. And it is the most important thing. Not what others think, not what you've been told. Not what might be acceptable. If you wish it, then it is yours to have. This thing between two people who desire each other…it is bigger than society. It is why people risk everything for a taste of it. It is why they risk their reputations, why they risk their marriages. Why they risk their futures. I have never understood why a man would risk his soul for power. For wealth. But in this moment, I can understand why a man would risk damnation for this.'

'No one makes these rules?'

And he could see that that was the exact right thing for her to think of.

'Remember I compared it to a waltz? I said just knowing the steps would never make it mean all that it does.'

'Yes,' she said.

'I was wrong to compare it to a waltz. That does not do it justice. Because a waltz has steps, and you can put one out of place. Because a waltz has observers. Because it has an element of performance. There is no performance here. If you wish to taste, then you taste. If you wish to scream, then scream. You do not have to wear clothes, your hair does not have to be arranged. We are, in this moment, closer to animals, I think. Or maybe closer to gods.'

She bit her lip at his moment of sacrilege, but she said nothing.

'Do you not think so, Aphrodite?'

'I think…I think you will have to remove your own clothes before I can decide.'

'Soon, I will have you do it for me. But as I'm certain you don't possess the hidden skills of a valet, I will not heap another unknown task upon you.' He stood back and began to make quick work of his cravat, his jacket, his waistcoat. When he removed his shirt entirely, Kitty actually did smile.

And he felt as though the sun had come out from behind the clouds.

Chapter Eighteen

Kitty might have felt foolish except…he had just given her permission to feel nothing of the kind. Because she felt herself grin the minute he shed his loose, white shirt, and exposed the heavy corded muscles of his chest, his shoulders. His waist was tapered, the muscles of his stomach brutally defined. She had thought that he seemed hard, like a mountain, and she could see now that she had been correct. She could also see that he appeared more closely related to granite than man. His body was a testament to hard labour, when it should not be. He claimed to be a man of excess, debauchery, and yet those men had a ruddy look to them. The blood vessels on their nose and cheeks closer to the surface, their bodies soft from indulgence. Men of leisure did not look like this. In fact, there were sparingly few men among the *ton* who weren't themselves egg-shaped, like that fateful ballroom itself, where her fate had seemed to unspool like a ball of yarn, and George Claremont had picked it up. Taking it in hand. As he did her now.

His body had hair on it. She found that fascinating. And beautiful.

He was dark where she was pale.

Rough where she was smooth.

Hard where she was soft.

And it ignited a hunger in her that far surpassed any craving for cake she'd ever experienced.

'What makes you smile?'

'I understand. Without knowing.' And it was true. She did.

She wasn't embarrassed to be standing in front of him with nothing on. Because he looked at her as if he was a cat and she was cream. And how could she wish to cover herself when a man gazed at her so intently?

How long had it been since anyone had seen her? Truly seen her. How long had it been since she'd been truly cared for? She was lucky enough to have friends in Hattie and Annie, but...

There was something in his gaze now that was like a salve for a wound she had only scarcely been aware of. And then he moved his hands to his boots, removing the sleek leather slowly, and she had to wonder if he took a care with where these clothes came from. Had to wonder if all that resentment that she had poured on him had been unfair.

But then his hands went to the falls of his breeches and she could think of nothing.

And when he was wholly exposed to her, that hard staff standing out proud from his body, large and decidedly not related to what she had seen on statuary, she could not think or speak.

He was a bronzed Hercules.

For in his glory, aroused and desiring her, he was the single most beautiful thing that she had ever seen.

His hard length jutted out away from his hard stomach, his thighs as hard as the rest of him. She wanted to touch him, but she didn't know where to begin. And she was relieved when he reached out and wrapped his arm around her, pulled her up against the length of his body so that she could feel him. Every inch of him to every inch of her.

The hair on his chest made the crests of her breasts ache, and she rubbed herself against him, trying to alleviate it. That slickness between her thighs felt more pronounced, as did the ache there.

All of it ached. Was it like this for everyone? Was it like this the whole time? She could not conceive of it. It was far too much, and not enough all at once.

She did not know what happened next, except she knew she wanted his mouth on hers again.

And then it was as if he'd read her mind, kissing her deep and hard as he moved his hands over her bare curves, as his palm came down to cup her buttocks, squeezing her, and then, his hand moved deeper between her thighs, touching the wetness there, and she jumped. It felt… A small whimper escaped her lips, and he continued to kiss her as he pushed his fingers deeper, the movement a tease. And then one finger was pushed deep inside her. And she gasped.

Nothing was wrong. He'd said as much. There could be nothing wrong between the two of them. He began to work his finger in and out of her body, and she rolled her hips in time with the movement. She didn't understand what was happening. Her breath came harder, faster, and he toyed with her with one hand between her legs, and gripped her chin with the other, licking into her mouth as he moved his finger inside. She pressed her hips flush against him, a tender, needy part of her rubbing against his thighs as he continued his siege against her.

She could feel something blooming inside of her. Could feel it building. 'George,' she whimpered.

'That's it,' he growled against her mouth. 'You'll find it. You'll understand.'

He pushed another finger in with the first and she cried out, something inside her releasing, a wave washing over her. Her muscles pulsed around his fingers, and she could not stand. If it weren't for him quickly wrapping his arm around her waist she would've collapsed to the floor. The pleasure that rioted through her was like nothing she had ever imagined. White heat streaking across her eyelids as she writhed then whimpered against him. She had found her pleasure.

Pleasure.

This was what it meant. There had been good food in her life, but it had not been this. There had been soft bedding, but it was not this. Every single thing she would've described as pleasure that she had experienced before this moment now needed another word. Needed something else.

Because this was pleasure. What he had said to her made sense now. As though a bell had been rung in her chest. In her whole being.

Suddenly, she was aware of all that her being encompassed. When before she had not been. For how could she be?

And then she found herself being laid down upon soft bedding, the world spinning.

'George,' she whispered.

She looked at him, and she had the sudden impression that she could see him. And it was the oddest thing, because of course she had seen him. But she felt before as though it was through a glass, and now it was as if there was no barrier between them at all. He was naked, and so was she, save for her stockings.

'I quite like the stockings,' he said. 'But when you wrap your legs around me, I should like to feel only your skin.'

It was as if he read her mind.

The words didn't quite make sense to her, but it didn't matter. She didn't need sense. She just needed George.

He was a rake, and a reprobate, she knew that. She didn't esteem him, and he didn't esteem her in the sense that he had mocked what she cared for only a few weeks ago in a ballroom, but none of that matched up with the man who loomed above her now, who kissed her tenderly before drawing one stocking off her foot, and then the other.

What she knew, she no longer knew. And what she had discovered in the last few moments painted the world an entirely different shade.

Kitty had always been very certain of herself. Certain that she understood things. In many ways, certain that she understood things with a greater depth than most other people around her.

She rarely questioned herself. Here right now, though…right now she did. Right now, she had no choice. How could she do anything but question herself. She had not known that feelings like this existed before George had taken her to his bed.

He slipped her other stocking off, and then he eased his body between her legs. She parted them for him, easily. She didn't know what he was doing. And actually, even that made sense now. To trust him. With this. With her own body.

He kissed her. Deep and drugging, and she felt the hardest part of him nudging against where he had put his fingers before.

That had felt good, but this part of him was much larger. And the idea of being breached by something quite so big made her know a moment of nerves.

'It may hurt,' he said. 'But only for a moment. And then you'll experience pleasure like you did before. Can you trust that? Can you trust me?'

She nodded mutely. 'Yes.'

'Good. Trust me, Kitty.'

The blunt head of him breached her, and then he thrust home with unerring swiftness. The invasion took her breath away. He was so large. So much larger than she had anticipated even.

And it felt… She felt as though it was too much. And yet, the idea of him drawing away from her made her feel bereft. She was a stranger to herself in this.

The world was strange to her. That magic. Beautiful.

She moaned as he began to move, as he withdrew slowly, and then thrust back. She put her hands on his chest, suddenly desperate to explore every inch of his body. She moved her fingers over his muscles. How had she never thought that a man's form could become her entire world? How could she have never realised what it would mean to be so close to someone else?

She darted her tongue out, licked the side of his neck. He tasted of skin and sweat and George. And she was wild for him.

He suddenly felt like the one true thing. The anchor of it all, holding her to earth. And she had no idea who she was.

Kitty Fitzroy had never thought of a man in such a fashion. Had never imagined such a thing might be possible. But Kitty Claremont wanted more of what her husband had shown her. She wanted everything. She wanted to feel that burst of pleasure again more than she wanted anything else. There were no cares within her right now. She did not feel a heavy weight. She felt nothing but desire. Nothing but need.

And then his movements became fractured, and she felt as if he were no longer showing her pleasure, but rather he was lost to it. Utterly and completely. A slave to sensation as much as she had ever been.

'George,' she said, gripping his shoulders, her fingernails digging into his skin as she felt need rise up inside her again. As she felt that same level of desire grip her as before, but this time, it came from somewhere deeper. The intensity absolutely stunning.

His movements became erratic, her desire for him a living thing, and she met each and every one of his thrusts, crying out as release overtook her again. And then, he found his own and he shook, that man made of granite trembled as his own need became too much for him to withstand.

The roar of pleasure only stoked her own desire, and she felt continual waves arcing through her as he took his own pleasure.

The morning light was bright, and George kissed her before moving away from her, withdrawing from her body. It all made sense. What he had said in the carriage. How you would do anything to be closer. As close as you could be. And the logical thing, after that, was to be joint, as they had been. If he would've told her, however, she would have expressed grave scepticism. He had been right. About that as well. That it was better for her to experience the need. Because then she had understood.

She touched his chest, fascinated by the way it looked, her hand against that part of him.

It was a strange thing, to spend so much time not being touched. Only to be touched so thoroughly. And to have permission to touch in return.

'Are you all right?'

'Yes,' she said, feeling dazed. 'Is that…is this what everyone knows? Is this what they all do? Hattie and the Earl and…'

'Yes,' he said slowly. 'However, I would say that the degree to which we both took our enjoyment was… It has never mattered to me, which woman I took to my bed.'

'You do have vast experience of this,' she said, feeling a pang in her chest. Why should she feel upset about that? She didn't want another person to touch him. Not at all. It made her feel ill. The thought of another woman putting her hands on him…

She felt inflamed with fury.

The idea that he had been on the verge of marrying someone else suddenly felt sharp. Had he been thinking of her? Had he wished that she was Helene? She hated this. Yes, being with him introduced new and interesting things, but each time they grew closer, it introduced something that hurt as well.

'Yes. But believe me when I tell you, each female body has been…much the same as the next. You create something different in me.'

The words sounded torn from him, and she did not quite know what they meant.

'Oh.'

'I shall have your maid come and draw you a bath.'

'Thank you,' she said softly.

She didn't want him to leave. She wanted him to stay, and yet…it made sense. A bath. And his departure. But she felt rather small and a bit tender. Both physically and around her heart. She swallowed hard and he took his leave, dressing slowly, and she could not quite help admiring his form as he did so.

She wanted to say something to him. She never had trouble with it in the past. In fact, words just seemed to fall out of her mouth when he was present. There was little that could be done about it. And now there were none. She was so confused. By the power of this thing.

And by how badly she wanted George Claremont to hold her. She was supposed to have more power. A title, and all of that. But at the moment she just felt small.

And some of her boldness had deserted her. Because would she not have simply asked him to stay before? But it felt like a risk now. One that she could not bear to take.

So she let him leave. Now she felt changed.

'There you have it, Kitty. You are yourself a wife. And altered because of it.'

And she no longer was ignorant. Of what the Duchess had spoken of, of what George made her feel.

And perhaps that was the real problem. She was crushed beneath the weight of the fact that she had wanted George Claremont in this way from the moment she had first laid eyes on him. The discomfort, the near animosity, all of it related to this.

But she was crushed also by the weight of the knowledge that he was still George Claremont, and every objection that she had ever had to him remained present and very real in spite of this new knowledge.

She wanted him. But he was not a man she could respect.

She wanted him. But he was not a man that she could love.

And did you want love, Kitty?

Yes. She had. Deep down, she had.

It was only now that she was facing the prospect of a life without it that she understood.

And she could not even curl into a ball and weep because a maid was on her way to draw a bath.

So Kitty did not weep. She simply remained stoic in the face of the unfairness of it all.

For what else was there to do?

Chapter Nineteen

George had not liked the way that Kitty had looked at him. Her eyes filled with soft awe.

As though he was something or someone he wasn't, couldn't be.

He wanted to be the man who'd held her tonight, but he was a man with a mission bigger than the both of them. A man whose hands were sometimes called upon for violence.

They'd had very little in the way of civil moments since they had first made their acquaintance. One remarkable, and notable time being that moment out on the terrace. He had been unguarded then because of the grief that had rioted through his soul. And when he had taken her this morning…

He had felt as though she had seen down into him in a way that was unconscionable. The way that he could not allow.

No. He could not.

It would compromise everything, and he had lived his whole life…

Already not marrying Helene disrupted things. Limited his access.

He could afford no more lapses in judgement. No more mistakes.

And so, he did not go to her that night. Instead, he went to Lily Bell's, and took a spate of new children to the children's hospital. He also spent time at the hospital, finding out where he might send the children that were there in residence.

Some of them had families to go back to, and they would need support so that none of them had to return to work in the factories. But some of them had nowhere to go, and they would need to go out to the place he was establishing in his country estate.

It was all in hand. He had everything in that programme beginning to run smoothly.

He knew that the doctor did not fully understand his aim. He was one of only two people besides those he hired out of his country estate, who had any idea about his involvement in such matters.

The other was Lily Bell.

He knew a moment of guilt over Kitty's ignorance.

The next day, Kitty was at breakfast early.

And he knew a tug of both guilt and desire looking at her sitting there, as beautiful as a rose. She was wearing pink. Her cheeks the colour of crushed petals.

Damn, but she was beautiful. He had not fully realised that until he had…until he had opened his eyes. He had known that he found her pretty, but she had stolen something from him yesterday when he had stripped her bare and entered her body.

She had stolen something that he did not think he could get back.

He prided himself on being utterly and completely unknowable to members of the *ton*, and yet Kitty made him want to reveal parts of himself.

He turned his mind away from that, and thought instead of how eager she had been. How perfect. She had not been shocked, and she had not been fearful. She had never once shrunk away from his touch. He had been correct. She was naturally passionate, and it transferred easily to physical passions.

A gift, he knew. And yet, it was not one he felt he should avail himself of.

But there she was. And he could see that she was eager. Eager for more.

'Were you after food this morning, Kitty? Or were you simply looking to offer yourself up to me as a treat?'

Her gaze snapped up to his.

'Speechless? That is unusual.'

'I find that since yesterday, there are a great many things that feel…rearranged inside of me.'

He felt the same. But he would not admit it.

It was only sex, after all. What was the point in getting bound up in these things? There was no point. He was adding weight to what happened between them, as if he were the virgin. Perhaps it was simply because she was one, and he found it intoxicating.

'Have you had a bath this morning?'

'No. I had one last night.'

'So you did. I was quite angry with myself for leaving, I must confess. I should've liked to have joined you.'

'Oh.'

'But…'

He rang a bell, and one of the servants came in quickly. 'Will you have a bath made ready in my chamber? We will not be requiring assistance.'

The maid nodded, and if she were shocked, did well at covering it. Kitty, in contrast, did not.

'Do you wish to bathe with me?'

She nodded slowly. 'I would… I think I would like it.'

'What is your objection?'

'No objection. Simply…I have never been aware of these kinds of things occurring between men and women before, and you act as if everyone in the house will be…'

'You have been protected. Kept away from the salacious realities of the world. But I promise you, this is not shocking behaviour.'

'I don't understand it. The way that young women are treated.'

'That is one thing that you have enlightened me on. For now, I do not understand it either. I had taken it as the way of things. But the way that you have highlighted it… You are correct.'

And there was more. Because of course Hannah had not been protected at all, because she was not a lady. And then there was Lily Bell. Who had not only been subjected to labour, and very nearly killed herself, but had then been forced to barter her body for protection for a great number of years, until George had managed to find her again.

There were some women who were not protected at all. Others who were protected to their detriment. Another truth of the world that would never make any sense to him.

'Really?'

She seemed shocked and delighted to have him say that to her.

'Yes. I confess, it is not something that I had fully considered before. But you are correct. It is absurd. The way that women are treated. Protected. It is not a protection, is it?'

'No. Though I should have got a lot less done on a day-to-day basis had I known these sorts of things occurred between people. My paintings, at least, should have had very different subjects.'

'Then you enjoyed it. What happened between us.'

'Yes,' she said, sounding breathless.

She was a puzzle, this woman, and he should not be quite so compelled to examine the pieces. For she was not his concern. Not really. He had never meant to have a wife who consumed his focus in any way. He had only ever meant to marry to serve his cause. But he had already decided that in terms of what Kitty would offer children, she could not be matched.

But it was what he felt for her that had no place. This… He had been honest with what he'd said to her after. It had never been quite like that for him.

For what they had was the sort of animalistic connection he'd heard people speak of before, but had not

entirely believed in its existence. He had thought that
it was an excuse for selfishness. A married man pro-
claiming to have an uncontrollable desire for a woman
he was not married to. He had always thought that sort
of thing a shield for bad behaviour, but he was married
to Kitty. She was his to do with as he wished freely.
And it had been far beyond anything he'd ever tasted
before, and now, he wanted her rather than breakfast.

He waited five minutes. And he assumed at that point
the bath would be ready, or they would not be taking
one.

'Let's go upstairs,' he said.

Kitty looked excited. Not so much in the way that
he would typically characterise this kind of excitement.
She looked as if he had offered to take her to a travel-
ling magic show.

She stood, and drew closer to him, pressing her
hands to his chest, and the expression was just so open,
so brilliantly sweet, that he had no defence against it. 'If
I kiss you here, darling, I will end up taking you across
the top of the breakfast food, and I don't think you, I,
or the cook wishes that to be so.'

'Oh,' she said. 'Does that mean we can't attempt to?'

'Yes,' he said.

He was so accustomed to bantering with women who
knew about sex, and when he spoke the words, they
were empty, but it was a game that all enjoyed. It could
not be a game with Kitty. It could never be. She was
far too sweet, and far too sincere. Sincerity. What did
he know of that? He had none of it in his life. He had
schooled it out of himself with great precision. For he

had cared once, wholly and entirely, he had loved his father without reservation, he had believed in the legacy of the duchy, and then he had discovered Hannah.

Hannah, who had been the sister he had not had. Hannah, who he had wanted to rescue. His father's blood, languishing in a factory because of his duplicity, and his unwillingness to be honest about his failings.

She had as much a right to live as he did… If she had no right to it, why did he? These rules. On that he agreed with Kitty. These rules. People died over the preservation of them. And even if not death itself, they lived miserable squalid lives striving to put food in their mouths while they worked themselves to the bone and…and people like himself were simply handed everything.

It disgusted him. Yes, he had cared once. But the cost was too big a burden. Getting up every day caring as he did…it was an improbability, and one he could not contend with. But Kitty deserved better. He just did not know how to give it to her. But he could give her pleasure. And he would be careful with the words that he used. He took her by the hand and led her from the dining room, and then lost patience and picked her up as he had done yesterday, carrying her up the stairs and down the hall. And she smiled up at him, a glow about her face. 'I like it when you carry me.'

And he saw emotion there that terrified him. For he was not equal to it. But what was to be done? She was his wife.

He opened the doors to the bedchamber and the maid was still in there, bent over the tub of water.

'That will be all,' he said. The maid scurried from the room, looking at the two of them, her cheeks red.

He began to strip his own clothes away, making quick work of them. He would teach Kitty how to undress him at some point, but for now he was impatient. She simply looked at him, her lips parted, her expression one of awe.

'They make so many rules all to contain this, don't they?'

'I find,' he said, removing his boots, his trousers, 'that there are rules to protect wealthy men primarily. Controlling women keeps them in charge. Controlling titles keeps them in charge. Controlling money keeps them in charge. If one controls desire, then one forces people to act in secret. One gives to others a gift of shame and fear. And so you see, that is the why of it. It is a simple thing. Basic. And yet it does not tell the truth. For people work beneath the surface of it, and they find that which they desire.'

'But we are here because of it.'

He looked her over. 'It's true. But I wanted you before. So you're aware. When I said that you were beautiful, I did not lie.'

'Then why were you going to marry Lady Helene?'

And here again, he couldn't speak the truth.

He had to protect his mission.

Or do you simply not wish her to know what you are? A bitter, twisted man who would have used a simple girl to get at her father? A man who has fought other men to the death, to save others, and yet the end result is the same. You are a man who, in your soul, might be no different than they are. Is it simply that you wish to hide that?

'Because marriage has always to me been less about desire and more about what you might gain from it. I would never have touched you, Kitty, because I could not give you what a woman in your position needs. And that, is society. But also, it is decent. A stark and true reality is that these sorts of things are more risky for women. You are the one that can be left with a child. And then the burden of care falls to you if men do not make a way for them. I do not play with women like you because the cost is potentially too great.'

'You said there were ways of preventing… You said that…'

'Yes. When you shatter, you know the feeling I mean, when you come… When men do that it can produce a pregnancy. But I can do it outside of your body. That helps with the risk.'

'Oh.'

'I didn't yesterday. Would you prefer if I did?'

She shook her head. 'It's fine.'

'Are you ready to have a child?'

'I…' Suddenly her expression went very soft. 'I am ready to not feel alone in the world.' It was a genuine, Kitty sort of answer.

'You're not alone.'

She looked up at him, her eyes luminous. 'I know that. I do. I have the Avondales, and I have Hattie and Annie, and I…'

'I will protect you,' George said.

She took a step forward, and he was completely

naked, the evidence of his desire for her impossible to hide—not that he would anyway. She put her hand on his face and looked at him. 'I don't understand how you are the man who picked up my yarn in that ballroom. I don't understand why you lie about who you are.'

He grabbed hold of her wrist and held her hand in place. 'Perhaps it isn't a lie. Perhaps both are real.'

'I don't understand.'

'One thing I noticed about you, very early, is that you have no mask to wear. And everybody else does. You understand that, don't you? Whatever they want, whatever they feel, whoever they might be screwing...' He saw her jolt, and realised she had made out the meaning of what he had said based on her lack of understanding the word, and the context. 'You don't see it. Not sitting around a polite dinner table, not doing a waltz. You say everything that you feel as if there is no cost of such a thing, and there is no one else in that room treating conviction so cheaply. They play games. It's why they're so obsessed with the lives of others. They hide what they feel, sometimes even from themselves. I do believe that some of them are as shallow as they appear, but others... They have whole lives we would never know about.'

'So it's a game,' she said. 'And I have not been treating it as such.'

'It's one of the things that draws me to you. You say all of the things that ought to be said, and you force those who have never thought about such things, or who do not care about such things to reveal themselves. You make them uncomfortable.'

'So do you.'

'Yes. But in a way that gives me power. I don't just know how to play the game, Kitty, I know how to control the game. And it is a very valuable skill.'

'To what end?'

'Right now?' For he could not answer about the future. For he could not give her honesty. 'This end. For now, there is nothing else.'

Slowly, achingly so, he removed her dress, leaving her body completely bare to his hungry gaze. He lifted her effortlessly and deposited her into the warm water, and he got in after her, over her. She lifted her hand and touched the side of his neck, down to his chest, her fingertips drifting slowly beneath the water, and then back up again, the skin meeting skin now slick with dampness. He lifted her and reversed their positions, bringing her over the top of him as he leaned back against the edge of the tub. She was over him, her small, beautiful breasts just there, and it was all he could do not to lean forward and take one into his mouth.

But he was allowing her to explore. Allowing her to direct. She moved her hands over his chest, his stomach, and then she found his staff, stiff and hard beneath the water, aching for her touch. She curled her fingers around him and squeezed, the expression of awe on her face enough to send him over the edge, and only years of practising restraint kept him from spilling then and there.

'Does it hurt?' she whispered.

'No,' he grunted. 'I'm trying to control myself. So it does not end quickly.'

'You made me feel those things. The shattering. More than once.'

'Yes. Women can do that. Men need…' He winced as she rubbed her thumb over the underside of his shaft. 'Time. Between. To get hard again. And I should not like you to have to wait for me.'

'I wouldn't mind.'

In truth, it would not take him very much time to become erect again after, not with her. He was certain of that.

But still. He was trying to be a gentleman. She was inexperienced, and she deserved for her pleasure to come first.

Funny how, for a man who had never been with a virgin before, he had a lot of opinions about how it should be conducted. About how it all should work.

Or maybe it was simply that he was greedy. For her desire. A longer time with her.

Right now, everything felt like a struggle. Fighting the battles he was embroiled in felt never-ending. And he was beginning to wonder if he was having any impact at all. And he despised himself for that. For growing weary. For growing hopeless. For there were any number of people counting on him to continue fighting. He did not have the right to these feelings.

But Kitty…perhaps this was the function she would serve. Because this was renewing. Invigorating. Because this reminded him of good things in the world. Or perhaps it just made him forget about the bad.

And very little had possessed the power to do that

since he was nine years old. It had been a struggle of twenty years, this burden he carried.

Her delicate fingers continued to explore him, moving over his body with tentative curiosity, and then with yet more boldness.

And then, he began to lose the battle. He moved his hands up to cup her breasts, teasing her nipples, and she gasped. Then he put his hand between her legs, and began to tease her, torment her, until it became torment too much to bear for himself. He lifted her up, his hands beneath her thighs, and leaned back just so on the tub so that he could bring the heart of her up to his mouth.

She gasped, gripping the edge of the tub behind his head. 'George!'

He feasted on her. On her innocence. Her desire. She struggled at first, but he held her fast, devouring her, pushing both of their need higher and higher. He was so hard he hurt. He wanted to drive into her, wanted to do something to alleviate his need. But his hands were busy holding her fast to his mouth, and he would not sacrifice the taste of her for anything. Not now.

She began to rock her hips against his mouth, and he shuddered with the depth of his need.

She was slick with her desire, and it was sweet as honey. And though she had made a show of modesty for a moment—he imagined it was ingrained, whether you had knowledge of this sort of act or not—she quickly gave in to her body's demands.

And this was what he liked about Kitty. She was altogether honest. About what she felt. About what she wanted. About who she was. His beautiful woman had no mask, and he felt envious, worried for her, and enchanted by it all at once. But now, in this moment, he did not have to wear a mask either. He could simply give in.

And he did.

He devoured her until she was shaking, until she had cried out her own release twice. Begun begging him to stop.

And then, he lifted her down, and poised her over his shaft, bringing her down slowly over him. Her wet heat was like a tight velvet glove, squeezing him tight as he entered her.

'George,' she said.

And he had the realisation then that she said his name freely when she desired him.

It hit him, square in the chest, the honesty of it.

He felt undone by her. Unequal to her.

'You know how to ride a horse, don't you?'

She nodded solemnly, and he did not have to say more. She began to move, in a rhythm not dissimilar to a trot. And then, a smooth gallop, higher, faster, driving them both insane. He held her head steady as she rode him, forced her to meet his gaze as she did, and he watched, as her eyes became clouded with need. With desire.

And then, her head fell back and she lost herself yet again. He kissed her, swallowing her cry as pleasure shattered her body.

And then he gripped her hips, lifting his own up to thrust deep as he brought her down hard over the top of him. 'I'm going to…'

She gasped, and then pleasure took her again, just as

it took him, and he spilled himself inside of her, growling as he did.

She went limp against his chest, moving her fingers in lazy circles.

'I was unaware that these things could be done in a bathtub.'

'You were unaware these things were done at all before yesterday.'

'What if I want to put my mouth on you?' she asked, her eyes direct.

He was still buried inside of her, and he could feel himself getting hard again.

'That is not typically an act a man asks of a lady,' he said.

He felt it was his duty to let her know that, at least. So that she did not think oral pleasure was a debt that had to be repaid.

'All right. But what if you're not asking me. And I'm asking you. Because I want to.'

'Kitty…'

'You said anything I wanted. You said there was nothing wrong. No rules.'

He huffed a laugh. 'So I did. And you're right. Between us, there are no rules.'

She nodded. Slightly clumsily, she removed herself from his body, and got out of the tub. She was naked and glistening, and he was well and truly hard for her again.

He watched as she dried herself, and then walked over to the bed. He followed her out of the tub, standing there looking at her back, the elegant curve of her waist, the dimples above her plump buttocks. He moved behind her and put his hand on her, squeezed her. And she squealed. Then turned, and saw him hard and ready again, her eyes widening. 'You said it took time.'

'Less time than anticipated,' he said.

Her eyes went determined, and then wicked, and because it was Kitty, he knew that it was not a show. No character put on to make him desire her. It was simply what she felt.

She looked him over, as if trying to do an extremely difficult equation. 'Sit,' she said.

'Sit?' he questioned, lifting a brow.

'On the edge of the bed.'

'All right.' He sat down on the edge, and she climbed up to the mattress beside him, on her knees. She looked down at his arousal with pointed curiosity, and then leaned in, flicking her tongue over the head of him.

'Kitty,' he ground out, and then a vile curse he should not have uttered as she parted her lips and took him inside. She seemed to have a fairly natural understanding of what to do, even if her movements were tentative. It did not take her long to take as much of him as she could into her mouth, stopping only when it proved to be too much.

'Sorry,' she said.

He cupped her cheek and looked down at her, at her flushed cheeks and swollen mouth. 'You have absolutely nothing to be sorry for.' It cost him to say that, because he barely had access to words of any kind. Because he was nothing more than need, nothing more than desire, pounding through him like a drum.

She wrapped her hand around the base of him, and continued to tease him with her mouth, and he felt his need roaring up inside him like a monster. There was nothing. Nothing but this. Nothing but her. There was no world outside of this room. Everything good was here, and nothing bad existed. For the first time in a very long time, he was blank of all things except need. Except pleasure.

'Kitty,' he said, by way of warning, but she continued to lick and suck him and he was only a man. He gave himself up to it, holding her fast as he found his release.

He felt weightless. Released. Given over entirely to this thing between them. Surrendering to an orgasm that surpassed anything else he'd ever experienced. And when he looked down at her, her cheeks were flushed, her eyes bright, her lips swollen.

'Kitty,' he said, cupping her chin. 'I'm sorry. I should have…'

'What?' she asked.

She sat up, and he could tell that she was dizzy by the unfocused look in her eyes.

'I am sorry. You are inexperienced. And I should've warned you. I should've pulled away from you before…'

'Why are you apologising? It was wonderful.'

'Wonderful?'

Of all the things, he had not expected that. Ever.

'It's…it's astonishing.'

'What is?'

'It's astonishing how much you can want another person. And how…how close you can be.' She yawned. 'I'm so tired.'

She had had at least four climaxes, and he was tired enough after his two.

'Lie down for a while,' he said, moving the covers back and gathering her to his chest.

She snuggled against him, her hands pressed to him, her legs tangled with his. 'You are right,' she said. 'It is the same as the waltz. Except if you explained the steps, I would've said that it sounded an indignity. An abuse. But it is nothing like that when…when the music overtakes you. And it feels a gift to be able to be so close to another person. To want to be. It is astonishingly wonderful. And it is…secret. Between us. Something that we share, that I don't share with anyone else. Of course, other women have done that for you, haven't they?'

He winced. 'Yes. But it is not the same,' he said. 'You can trust that.'

'Can you explain to me what's different?'

'I thought you were tired, Kitty.'

'I am,' she said. 'But…I feel as if I am looking up into the night sky, and suddenly there are so many more stars than I ever imagined. The dimension of it is astonishing. You're right, society's rules, the right and the wrong of it, it doesn't explain this. It does not explain the way that it all makes sense when you're caught up in the glory of it all. It could never make sense if you simply gave instruction on what could be done. You must feel it.'

She yawned and burrowed more tightly against him. And he waited for her to fall asleep. But sleep proved elusive for him, and in any case, he had no time for it. He had to balance the ledgers for the business, and he needed to check in on the newest imports, and the sale thereof. He also had another route to chart for the merchant ships. There was always much to be done. He might've felt for a moment as though the world did not exist, but the stark truth was that it did. And as much as he had enjoyed his time with Kitty, this morning's adventures were at an end. He had work to do.

But he gave a small amount of thanks that there was somewhere soft for him to return to when he had a moment.

Yes. He had finally figured out what good his marriage to Kitty did.

And she seemed of the same mind.

It was not half so disastrous after all.

Chapter Twenty

Kitty spent the next few days in a sensual haze. She still knitted, of course, and had her socks sent down to the hospital. She had seen Hattie and Annie twice and had done her best not to blush, as if they would be able to see the changes in her.

Instead she'd engaged them in a spirited political discussion over tea.

But George now occupied a place in her mind that felt large and significant in a way nothing except a cause ever had before.

George taught her things that she had never known existed, and it was all becoming part of the new vocabulary that she had not even known she had the scope to learn.

She felt confident in herself and everything that passed between them, because he was such an enthusiastic participant in the entire thing. And she found she did not have a limit to the desire that she experienced for him. There were not words. Not really. She had been slightly embarrassed, but struck by how profound it had felt, to take him into her mouth and to swallow down the evidence of his desire. To take him into her body as she did. And all the different ways it could be done. She knew that people treated it as a dirty secret. That it was something shameful. And yet, she could not feel any shame for what happened between her and George. It felt rather a benediction. And perhaps that was a sacrilege, but she could not bring herself to feel that it was.

She had been alone for so very long. She had felt alone. And there was something here, something in this that made her feel truly, wholly understood. Cared for. He made her body feel glorious. And he made her feel beautiful. And she had never thought she cared about such things, but with him, she did.

The days bled together, but he did not stay with her when they were through making love. And then one night, she saw him leave. She had suspected as much. That he left at night.

There was no… He could not still be seeing his mistress, surely?

Before, when she had heard that George kept a mistress and a town house, she had not fully understood what that meant. But now she did. Kissing. Bodies entwined together. Being inside another woman. She could not fathom such a thing. Another woman's mouth on what belonged to her. For she did feel that. That George, and every part of him, belonged to her.

How can you even think that? The two of you never have a real conversation. You have talked about desire and passion and society. And you still know nothing of him.

That wasn't true. She knew his father had disappointed him. She knew that he carried a heavy weight, and she knew that he felt he had to wear a mask. That he was certain everyone did. She could not say what that meant, but she knew those things. And yet, there were days that she passed him in the hall, and she felt as if she lived with a ghost or a stranger. A man she could not quite see. When they were together, in his chamber, and they had no clothes on, she felt as if they were the only two people in the entire world. She felt as if he understood her in ways she did not, and there was truth to that. For he knew what made her body tremble and quake, and had known it far before she had.

It was a strange thing, physical intimacy. For it made her feel achingly close to him, made her feel wildly attached to him, and yet…when they were not together, it also made her question.

Which man he was, really. And she could hear from him all he wanted that they were the same man. The one who had mocked her for knitting socks.

Her socks. She had not knitted half so much since coming to be with George. It was as though she was forgetting herself. Getting lost in all of these things concerning her and her feelings. Really for the first… for the first time since her father died.

She did not know whether to laugh or cry about that.

But George was leaving. George left every night. She did know that. In her heart she had. Was he going to see his mistress? She had to know.

So she would follow him. Because what wife wouldn't?

It didn't matter that he'd made no romantic declaration to her. It did not matter that she wasn't his choice.

She was his wife. There was no category for wife, other than wife. He was bound to her in front of God, and did that not matter?

She hadn't thought it would, but then she had thought George to be a silly playboy who could not compel her to feel anything when he…he made her feel everything.

She was filled with turmoil. She should not care where he was going, in fact, she should be grateful that he had given her reprieve, and yet instead she felt as if anticipation had been drawn out into something untenable. And then there was the fact that she was consumed with knowing where he was going.

She spoke to the housekeeper about her going out alone.

'My lady,' the housekeeper said. 'It is not advised.'

She looked at Mrs Brown and tried to beseech her. As one woman to another. She had no practice with such a thing but she hoped the other woman might look at her with understanding.

'I wish to know where my husband is off to.'

And she could see that the housekeeper had no real loyalty to George, which spoke volumes.

'Lady Curran…'

'I am an excellent rider. I was not raised here in the city. I spent all my days on the back of a horse as a child.'

From the look on her face, Mrs Brown likely thought that George was indeed being unfaithful. With a mistress. Just as Kitty did. And she knew now, vaguely, what it meant. That there would be no clothes, that he would be kissing her, and the way that he had just done Kitty.

He would kiss her everywhere. Make her tremble.

Make her feel as though she was the only one.

And Kitty ought not to care. Except… If he expected that he was ever going to come to her bed, then she could not have him occupying the bed of another woman. On that she felt quite clear. Even if she was unclear about other things.

She followed him at a distance. He was in that same closed, shiny black carriage that he had taken from the church after their wedding. It felt a curse. Sacrilege.

She saw it stop in front of a town house. And he got out, going to the front door.

And she could see a woman answering the door. And something in her went dead.

She was dizzy.

He was there. He was there with that woman. How could he? How could he do that to her? Of course, he had never promised her anything. He had never promised fidelity. But the way that he spoke to her, about how what they had was different. Is that what he told every woman? Including the beautiful, buxom blonde that had answered the door. She was far more beautiful than Kitty, and George might have said that Kitty was beautiful, but did he even mean it?

She felt violently ill. And part of her wanted to storm inside and stop whatever was happening and part of her…

That was what Kitty would've done before.

Everyone has a mask.

A mask. If she went in now, he would know. He would know that improbably, her heart was affected by this. That she had taken what passed between them in bed, in the bathtub, on the floor, against the wall, to mean something more than what it was. That she had begun to feel...

As though he was family. Or something else.

You were beginning to fall in love with him. And that is a foolish thing.

It was. It was only a foolish thing, because she did not know this man. She knew nothing about him. Nothing at all. And simply because he made her body sing, she had been foolish enough to believe that it was love.

But of course it wasn't.

And she could not expose herself that way. She could not let him know what a fool she was. What a blessedly silly child. She could not let him know.

And so she turned the horse around. Went back to the town house, and closed the door. And only when she was safely in her bedchamber did she begin to weep.

She cried until she was wrung out, but then, with her face still wet from tears she asked herself what had become of her father's daughter?

Fighting for what she was passionate about was her gift. She did it at dinner tables and in ballrooms. It was who she'd been as a debutante. She had to be the same as a wife.

She would fight for her husband.

And she would win.

Chapter Twenty-One

When Kitty found George in his study hours later, he was slumped in his chair. His cravat was undone, his shirt part way open. He had a cut on his face. Had that been part of a game of passion with his beautiful blonde mistress? It made her ill to think of.

How could he share what they had with someone else?

And she felt inside of her breast a passion, and anger, that matched any she had ever felt about the injustices of the world. Because this was an injustice. George had made her want him. George had consumed her, had made her care about him on equal footing with her cares of the world, all while being an insensible rake. And it was not fair. She stepped into the room, and he looked up. 'Kitty…'

'George.'

'It's late. Why are you up? And why are you dressed?'

'A question that I might ask you.'

'You know how it is.'

'No. I don't, George. Or rather, I don't know why.'

He was hers. His body was hers, his mouth was hers. She wanted...she wanted more than that to be hers. And she could not understand why. Except that he was not what he showed the world, and she knew it. He wasn't what he showed her, and she wondered sometimes if he was what he showed himself.

She could do nothing else.

She crossed the space to him, and she put her legs astride his thighs, on the chair, leaning in and claiming his mouth for her own. 'You are mine, George Claremont,' she said. 'And this is a reckoning. I do not care where you were tonight. And I will not ask. But you are mine. From this day forward. We said vows under duress. We were forced to make promises that you never intended to keep. But you will promise me now.' She pressed her thumb to his lips and smoothed it over to the corner of his mouth. 'You are mine.'

And she had never felt so much conviction, not even when she lectured an entire ballroom full of people about labour practices. Because she would have this. She would have him.

'Take me,' she begged. 'Make me yours. In truth.' He reached up and grabbed the back of her hair, drawing her head down to his with force. The kiss was angry, grinding their lips together, and she could feel his teeth scrape against her mouth.

She bit him. And he growled. 'Do not treat me as though I am fragile. Do not treat me like a virgin bride. I can be whatever you need.'

He tore the front of her dress. Rent it in two. And

then her chemise next, baring her breasts to his gaze. He was like an animal. He pressed his mouth to her neck, biting her there, sucking, before moving down to her breasts and taking one nipple deep within his mouth, and he bit that as well. She gasped.

Their lovemaking had verged on violent before, but this crossed into new territory. They were wild with each other. Angry. She clung to his shoulders as he suckled her, her nails digging into his skin. 'Yes,' he growled. And it was as though all the anger that existed inside them, at each other, at the world, exploded into an inferno of passion. He tugged her hair, forcing her head back, licking the column of her neck before nipping her jawline, her chin. He reached between them, undoing the falls of his breeches, and exposing his cock, finding the damp centre of her beneath her layers, and thrusting up inside her. He held her hair still as he set a punishing rhythm.

It hurt. The ferocity with which he thrust into her. But she craved it. Wanted more of it. It made her feel as though there was something. Something bright. Something real. It made her feel as though she was grounded to this moment. Grounded to him. As though, finally, all of his feelings and all of her feelings had melded into one. This passion, this angry, brilliant passion that they carried around inside of them. And it exploded between them. Maybe, just maybe this was the key. To them being everything.

Her orgasm gripped her, intense, shattering. And she cried out, her fingernails digging deep into his flesh, leaving score marks behind. And when he found his own release, his grip on her was bruising, punishing. And he left behind marks of his own that she knew she would later treasure.

She collapsed against his chest, tears forming in her eyes.

'You're mine,' she said weakly.

And he gathered her to him as though she was a tragic kitten, and carried her to her bedroom in spite of her ruined dress. She could not even bring herself to have a concern for a member of staff seeing them.

He stripped her naked and laid her down beside him in bed.

And he said nothing. He simply held her.

'You're mine,' she repeated.

'Yes,' he said, his voice rough. 'I promise.'

The next day, they did not speak of the storm that had overtaken them the night before. And she did not press for details on what had happened between him and the other woman the night before. But when he left her bed that night, something in her fractured. She did not follow him. It was possible that he was breaking things off with her. But possibly he was not.

And Kitty, who was not one to dwell in worry or misery for herself, gave in to tears.

Chapter Twenty-Two

It had been another night like any. He had gone down to the factory district to sabotage machinery, and that was when he'd seen it. There was a child. A little girl. She was struggling to get away from her captors, and one had struck a blow to her head that had sent her reeling backwards.

He knew exactly what sort of men they were. And exactly what sort of design they had on the child. This had nothing to do with the factories, but it was another symptom of all the evil out there.

And George would have none of it.

He drew his gun from the innermost part of his jacket and held it up on the men. 'Leave the child.'

'And who are you?' one of the men asked.

'Death, if you take so much as one step towards her or me. Go.'

And with absolute certainty, he realised something. That they were not going to allow him to get out of this without making the choice, and even if they did, it mattered not. Because they were not worth the air they breathed. Because they would do what they were doing to this child to many more.

And so when they advanced upon him, one with a knife, and the other with a gun, George took decisive action. The sound of the shots exploding in the alleyway could've woken the dead, but they did not rouse the child.

He bypassed the bodies of her captors and picked her up.

She was young. Ten maybe. Eleven. So very like Hannah.

He held her to his chest, and got on to the horse, riding back towards his home as though the hounds of hell were after him. He would not chance even stopping at Lily Bell's. He needed to be at his house, and he needed to send for a doctor immediately.

He had lost a little girl to her machinery injuries less than a fortnight ago, and he could not bear another innocent child being lost. Not now.

It did not matter what his own household thought. Nothing mattered. Nothing mattered but saving this child.

He rode as though the very hounds of hell were on his heels, and when he arrived at the town house, his man met him outside.

'See that the horse is put away. And send for a doctor.'

He went into the house and began barking orders. He needed hot water. Cold water. He needed to examine the child.

He had some basic knowledge of how to treat injuries, because doing what he did, it was an important thing. He felt as though he was being watched, and he looked up, and saw Kitty standing in the doorway. Her eyes were swollen and red-rimmed, her expression one of fury.

'You're back,' she said.

'Yes,' he said. And he realised that he would have to explain. Before he could open his mouth, Kitty stepped into the room and looked down. 'Oh. What has happened?'

'I found her,' he said, finding it best to leave out the details of what had transpired.

'You found her where?'

'I don't have time to explain, Kitty. I have sent for a doctor.'

'Why were you out?'

'Kitty…'

'No. I need to understand. Because I followed you the other night, George. I followed you, and I saw you go into your mistress's house.'

Dammit. Of course she had followed him.

'Lily Bell is not my mistress,' he said.

There was no point. There was no point to any of it.

'What?'

'I'm not who you think I am.'

It was time. Because he could not bear the look on her face, because this child was dying, because there was no putting this to rights without the truth coming out, and at the moment, it was immaterial. An important one.

'I don't understand.'

'I told you. Everyone in society wears a mask, it is only that mine is more pronounced. But I need your help. We need to clean the wound and stop the bleeding. She's hit her head. And she's unconscious. I've seen head injuries like this before. There may not be anything a doctor can do. Sometimes people simply do not wake up.'

'Tell me where you were.'

'In the factory district. I…I was there because I hate them too. I hate them too, and it is my life's work to stop the abuse of children in them. You know about the sabotage that's been happening?'

'I've heard about it. Yes.'

'I'm the one who does it.'

'George,' she said. 'You didn't tell me. You know that I feel the exact same way about this. And you let me— you let everybody think that you care about nothing.'

'Because I cannot have anyone knowing, Kitty. If people were to suspect…'

'It's why you have not gone to Parliament.'

'If I was bringing up legislation to champion laws against child labour, and to put restrictions on the work that they are forced to do, do you not think that my actions would be more greatly scrutinised? It is not something that I could countenance.'

'But you found this girl.'

'Unrelated to the factories. The kind of men I found her with are the type who use children for… They were likely going to sell her to a brothel.'

Kitty looked stunned. 'She's a child.'

'Yes. And some people will pay more for that, Kitty.'

'George…'

'This is what I wish to protect you from. You are overwhelmed already by the different travesties that occur in the world. The only thing I can do is teach you about more.'

'You do your best to stop it.'

'Come here.'

She came alongside him and without being asked, tore strips off the bottom of her nightgown and pressed them against the child's head wound.

'We will need liniment.'

'Is it on its way?'

He nodded.

'She can go to the infirmary. They will take care of her there.'

'I'm well acquainted with the doctor. I have brought him a number of children, but I did not feel that I could chance the trip with her. I wanted to get her off the horse as quickly as possible.'

'George. What happened to the men who were taking her?'

He opted not to answer that.

'George. What happened to them?'

'They engaged me in a fight. I had no choice but to make sure that it ended there. I am sorry if that bothers you.'

'All of this bothers me. But you doing what you must in a bid to make sure she's safe…in a bid to make yourself safe, that does not bother me.'

'I'm sorry,' he said again. 'I fear that I'm embroiling you in something that is beyond what I wished. There is little to be done. As accomplished a liar as I am, even I am not going to try to come up with a reason for this beyond the truth.'

'George, you…you really are not who I thought you were, are you?'

'I'm sorry,' he said. 'I feel as if you of all people did not deserve to be caught up in my lies.'

'Why didn't you tell me? Because you know that I am sympathetic to your causes.'

'It is not that simple.'

There was suddenly a commotion, and in came the butler, with a doctor not far behind. The director of the children's hospital quickly crossed the room and looked down at the girl.

'What happened?'

George recounted the story as quickly as possible. Down to what they had done so far to try to address the wound.

'I have brought a carriage; I can take her comfortably to the hospital.'

'I…' George felt torn by this. 'Keep me abreast of her condition. In the meantime, I will endeavour to find her family. If there is one. If she wakes and gives you a name, that would be yet more helpful, but until then I will use my contacts in Cheapside to find out if anyone is missing a daughter.'

'You have such faith in these matters. My assumption would be that it was her family who sold her,' the doctor said. 'People get desperate.'

'Yes,' George said. 'Some people do get desperate.'

And then there were men like his father who simply wished to protect their reputation. It was not about anything beyond their own comfort and never would be. Their own needs.

The doctor picked up the little girl and carried her out the door.

'Will she be all right?' Kitty asked, and he felt... at sea.

'I don't know. There was a child... The night of the ball, Kitty, when you saw me standing out on the terrace, there was a child who was injured in a factory accident. She was brought to Lily Bell's. Lily Bell's is a safe house for children. A stopover. She cares for them until I can find a place for them. Some people know. The child was brought to her, and before we could get the doctor, or take her to the hospital, she perished from her injuries.'

'Oh...'

'This is what happens when you involve yourself in the evils of the world. When you try to right wrongs, you are certain to see even more wrongs. Kitty, I feared that you knowing would put you in danger.'

'How?'

'If you knew what I did, and you were to say something to the wrong person, at the wrong dinner...'

Her brows locked together. 'You don't trust me.'

'No. I do not trust the world. The *ton* is full of men who know how these children are treated and who do nothing, who actively participate. I am able to move among them, to gain information, because they talk in my presence. But I have also done things to destroy them and if they found out, I would be in danger. You would be in danger.'

'I'm not a girl. And I care very deeply about changing the world. I do.'

'I can see that.'

'She really isn't your mistress? I feel certain that at a time such as this that is a trivial concern, but I cannot… George, I cannot bear it. When I saw you go into her house I felt as if…'

'She's not my mistress.'

'How did you come to know her? And why does everybody think that she is your mistress?'

'I will have tea brought for us. And you had best sit down.'

'But, George…it's late.'

'The housekeeper was already up fetching supplies to take care of the child. We might as well have some tea.'

'All right.'

They sat in the sitting room. And she was still in her torn nightgown. He offered her his coat, which she draped over herself. 'I guess the doctor saw me like this.'

'He's a doctor. And anyway. You're a married woman now. Practically impervious to scandal.'

'Yes. I suppose so. Tell me. Tell me everything.'

'As soon as we get our tea.'

When the tea was served, Kitty sat there, staring at her husband. Trying to make sense of what she knew of him. Somehow, this version of events made much more sense than anything she had previously known. Somehow, this seemed right. This seemed to be the truth of it.

Because she knew that George was not the feckless playboy that he pretended to be. Was not the scandalous rogue who cared for nothing. She had sensed his intensity, beneath the surface. And then there was the way that he treated her. The gravity with which he spoke of certain things. No. She had known for some time that he was not everything he appeared to be. And this made more sense. But there was a calculated façade that he kept in place for a reason.

George was a vigilante. His behaviour could wind him up in prison. Though, she knew it was unlikely given his status. It was still possible. Especially if he went up against men who were powerful enough. And the men who owned factories, the ones who invested in them… He was playing a dangerous game.

'I told you,' he said, 'I discovered that my father was not who I thought he was when I was nine years old. That was when I found out about Hannah. My half-sister. Her mother wrote to my father beseeching him for funds. She said that Hannah was having to go into the factory to work, as was she. My father threw the letter away, but I found it and I read it. It was upon reading that letter that I decided that I would go and find them. I found the factory. And eventually found Hannah. In a small way, I was able to know her. I started by bringing her treats from the kitchen.'

'How did you sneak away to the factories?'

'I was very good at evading my governess, and this was when I was home from school. I think they assumed that I was off getting into the kind of trouble that young boys did. They certainly did not think that I was out making the acquaintance of my half-sister. But I loved her. Quite instantly. And I could not understand why she was such a secret. One day she took me into the factory. She showed me the working conditions. I spent part of the day with her, working on one of the machines.'

'You did?'

'Yes. I saw a boy injured that day. He lost his finger. It was appalling. I'd had no idea… I had no idea.'

'This doesn't end well, does it?'

He shook his head. 'There was a fire. There was a fire and everyone working in the factory died. There is even a rumour that the manager barred the door to keep them all in. Let them perish with the goods so that they would be owed no kind of compensation. I don't know if that is true. If it was, rest assured I would track that man down myself, and I would make him accountable in ways that would keep you up at night.'

'George…'

'That was how I found out Hannah was gone. Arriving to see the factory a smouldering ruin. And they told me…no survivors. None at all.

'But there was another girl who was friends with Hannah. Her name was Lily Bell. She worked in a different factory. I spent years looking for Lily Bell. And when I found her, she too had fallen on hard times. I ended up putting her up in a town house, and this started the rumour of her being my mistress. She isn't. She never has been. She is someone that I have protected.

I would never take advantage of a woman that I was caring for in that capacity. You must know that. You must understand it.'

'I do now, George.'

'I care very deeply for her, but it is as a family member. She's a wonderful person. And she helps me with the children. She and I both do it as a tribute to Hannah. And we do our best to keep my name away from the entire thing. But my country estate…my country estate is something like a school. We take the children who do not have families, or whose families cannot care for them, and they go there.'

'Like an orphanage?'

'Perhaps. But…different. It is run so that the children feel as if they have a home. Feel as if they have a place. They are educated, and they are given skills. So that they can get different jobs later. But while they are children…they can be children.'

'George…this is…how do you afford such a thing? Everyone thinks you're living off your father's purse strings.'

'And again, they're wrong. I have a merchant shipping business where I make sure I purchase items not acquired via slave labour. But there are farms, where people work, and they are paid. On land that they can own. We take the goods, and import them here, where everything is manufactured safely and without the labour of children. It is expensive. But I have found a way to make money that way. It can be done. It can be done with a bit of care.'

'You work,' she said.

For there could be nothing seen as more disgraceful by the aristocracy.

'Yes. It is not a shameful thing to work, it is a shameful thing to sit around and accept things as they are. I personally am appalled by the behaviour of people who consider themselves my peers. It is wrong, the way they behave. Extremely wrong.'

'George, you're only one man. It seems as if you're fighting this from every angle.'

'I'm trying.'

'What, you mean to do it alone?'

'Again, being circumspect about who knows my thoughts on these things is important. For reasons such as tonight. Two men are dead, Kitty, and there was no other option, because it was me or it was them, you understand.'

'Yes.'

Her heart was thundering hard. She had no idea what to make of this news. This news that her husband was… an entirely different person than she had thought.

'Your hands are rough,' she said, a hint of wonder in her tone.

'Pardon me?'

'Your hands are rough. I thought that the night you put your hand beneath my dress. That your hands felt very rough for a man who had not done any sort of manual labour. But you do. It's a giveaway, George. As was the way that you treated me out on the terrace. You were good to me. And I…I felt very much that you were a man who had understood loss.'

'I will never get over that. My grief for Hannah will

never be diminished. There is no way. The unfairness of it…' His voice went rough. 'My parents are married. Her mother and my father were not. And that somehow made her beneath his notice. It made her beneath his care. And that told me everything I ever needed to know about him. I mattered only because I am the heir. It is the only thing that matters to the Claremont family. That they are able to carry their name forward.

'If I had been the bastard child, if I had been born on the wrong side of the sheets, you can rest assured that I would've been left to die in much the same way that she was. It is only this idea of blood, and bloodlines. It is only these farcical rules that made my father take me into his home. He was well able to forget about his other child. It is not simply that he did not love her, it is that he did not extend basic care to her as most people would to a sad, stray dog on the streets. She died because of his negligence. I loved her, but it was not enough to save her. I had no power. I was a child.

'And what is the purpose then, of all of this? These are the questions that you ask all the time, Kitty, and you are wrong about none of them. Why do men make these rules and subject themselves to them? But the answer is that it's men like my father who are not playing by the rules. They established them for everyone else and then they work around them. And there is a body count.'

'George, I'm sorry.' Because it was all she could say. She felt as if she were bleeding. She knew what it was like to lose family. But her father was a good man. A good man who had taught her by example. George had been tasked with finding what good was. Because his father had not modelled it. Not in truth. It was only that empty, shallow vision of propriety that society was so fond of.

'There is no need to be sorry. Not to me. But, knowing what I do, you can see that if I did not act it would be criminal.'

'I think it is criminal that no one else seems to act. I want to help you, George. I wish to go down to Lily Bell's immediately.'

'It is…it is a harsh reality, Kitty.'

'I know. I have known. I've been to the infirmary, I volunteered there with Hattie. I've been frustrated with the genteel ways that I have been allowed to participate in helping. I want to do something real.'

'You are far and away not what I expected a wife to be.'

'Well, I do not mean to completely defy your expectations.'

'It is just as well.'

She frowned. 'Why did you want to marry Helene Parks?'

He paused for a long moment.

'Her father owns a number of factories. I had thought the best way to begin to deal with the issue would be to be on the inside of it. I could know everything there was to know about the factories, tour them. And I could search his ledgers, find every child, find their families. And I could save them. And destroy him.'

'You wanted to marry her to get to her father.'

'Yes.'

Kitty's heart squeezed. That hurt her. It wasn't that she didn't agree with George when it came to his hard stance on these things—she felt the same issues keenly—it was only that…Helene didn't know. She would've been married to a man who in many ways despised her. Who was simply using her.

'But poor Helene is not her father,' Kitty said.

'And she did not end up marrying me. Do not worry, she would've been using me as well. There was quite a bit about her that I did not know, and that suited her. I think that she would have happily married to cover up her… Let's just say I believe that there were dalliances with other men. And I would've happily looked the other way.'

'That's another thing,' Kitty said, feeling the need to follow this opportunity to delve into the topic. 'I do not wish for you to be with anyone else.'

'I'm sorry?'

'I told you. When I followed you the other night I felt as if the world had gone sideways. I cannot bear the idea of you being with another woman, George. I will not allow it. I will wage war for you if I must.'

'Kitty, are you jealous?'

She thought about it. 'Jealous.' She tasted the word, as she had never had a chance to apply it to herself. 'Yes. I would say that I am. I would say that I am an extremely jealous sort. I want you to belong to me. And only me. I…' She was still trying to grapple with what she knew. 'When you've gone away every night it's been to see about business with the children?'

'Yes.'

'And you mocked me for knitting socks for the children.'

'I didn't mean it.'

'You lie very effortlessly,' she pointed out.

'It has been a necessity for me. To live.'

'What do you intend to do? With the duchy, with everything?'

He sat back in his chair. 'I thought about it for a long time. I thought about finding ways to get rid of the entail on the property to see if there was a way that I could alter the line of succession and ensure that it was all left to a society, a charity. But that is not so simple a thing. And I thought…I then thought that perhaps the easiest and best thing to do would be to have children who shared my vision.'

'They will,' said Kitty. 'I know that your father did not give you this burning desire to see justice. But mine did. And it is a part of him that I carry forward.'

'Nothing will ever be more important to me than this,' he said. 'You will have no trouble extracting fidelity from me, Kitty. Rumours of my proclivities have been greatly exaggerated. A man hardly has time to conduct endless affairs when he is attempting to dismantle the atrocities of the world.'

'I understand that. I…' Kitty realised that for the first time in her own life, she had been quite consumed by her feelings. Her comfort. Her body. She had spent so much time denying that. Concerning herself with everything around her. But the way that George had taken her and made her his had changed the way she thought about things, and it was quite…unexpected.

She did not dislike it. Only it made her feel a bit small and shallow, particularly when George was speaking of his causes the way that he was.

She had got distracted. He clearly would never allow himself to be.

'There's nothing to be done tonight,' George said.

And suddenly, he looked exhausted.

'I will draw you a bath.'

'No,' he said. 'There's no need.'

'Let me.' Because suddenly it wasn't simply enough to dismantle the unfairness in the world, she wanted to lift the burdens off George's shoulders.

She carried the water up and down the stairs, working to get the bath ready for him. She was not afraid of work.

And then, she took his hand and led him up to his chamber.

She had paid attention every time he had undressed, and when she went to divest him of his clothes, her fingers were nimble. She discarded everything and guided him to the tub. She knelt down on the outside of it, and felt gratified when he groaned and laid his head back against the edge of the metal trough.

She put her hands in the warm water, and bathed his chest, his shoulders. She kneaded at his tight muscles, and explored the lines on his face. 'Oh, George,' she said, looking at him now with entirely new eyes. Or perhaps, the same eyes. But a different context. Because she had thought that what she knew about him did not match, and she had been correct. George…

He was a hero.

And her heart felt full to bursting, because she had known. She had known that this man was something more. That he was something beautiful and brilliant. That he was worthy of affection, but now she had to look at him and know that he was a hero.

All the things that she talked about, he was out there doing. Physically putting himself in danger in order to effect the changes that she believed in.

He had lost. He had loved his sister, she could see it. He was loyal. And he had a strong sense of right and wrong. He was just so very different than she had believed.

And…somehow, she had felt it. And yet again, it all seemed to go back to the waltz.

Somebody could explain it to you. But unless you felt it, you would never know. She had felt George Claremont's goodness. When she had got beneath the caustic manner with which he dealt with everything, she had seen him.

And even though she hadn't been told all of the steps he had taken to become an extraordinary man, she had simply sensed that he was one.

She could see that he was exhausted, and so was she. So when he got out of the tub, she simply led him to bed, undressed herself, and got beneath the bedclothes with him.

He grunted, and pulled her against him, burying his face in her hair.

He didn't kiss her. Did not try to touch her intimately. He simply held her.

And she gloried in being held.

And somehow, all of the pieces felt as though they had come together. They had this sensual knowledge between them, but now there was something more. Tonight he had needed her, and she had been there. Tonight he had told her the truth. Of everything.

And now she felt as if they were united. No longer was she confused by how deeply she felt for him. It was just that she had clearly always known.

Kitty Fitzroy was quite certain she'd been made for George Claremont in that moment.

They cared. They cared so much they led with it in their souls. Always and for ever. But she did not know what that meant for a marriage. Not truly.

But they could hold one another.

And that had to be better than not being held.

Chapter Twenty-Three

When they woke in the morning, she was lying beside him. That was new.

George got up and dressed, and by the time he had tied his cravat, Kitty had begun to stir.

'You're awake,' he said.

'Yes,' she responded.

'I'm going to the infirmary to check on the child.'

'I'll go with you.'

'You've been to the children's hospital before?' he asked.

'Yes. Many times. With Hattie. You know she spent quite a lot of time in a doctor's care after she was thrown from her horse.'

'Yes. I do remember that.'

'Why do you ask?'

'I simply wanted to make sure that you were prepared. It is not necessarily the easiest place to be.'

'I already know that. But thank you. You don't need to protect me, George.'

'But I feel as if I should.'

'That's very kind. I'm not naive, though. Not about these things. Even if I might've been naive about what transpired between men and women,' she said, sliding out from beneath the covers and revealing her entire naked body to him.

Lust kicked him square in the stomach.

The depth to which he could feel desire for her, even with all of what was happening around them…stunned him.

He was not accustomed to thinking of his physical needs while being consumed with these other things. But with Kitty it seemed to always be happening, all the time. It was her. Always. Ever on his mind.

'I just never took the time to think about…my own body. And therefore, I did not quite understand certain things. But I do now.'

'And you feel happier for it.'

She looked thoughtful for a long moment. 'No. I feel that happiness speaks to a lightness. I do not feel light. I feel…worried about things that I never was before. But also conscious of a great many wonderful things that I had no knowledge of previously. It's very difficult to say whether or not it's happiness. But I feel that it's fullness. And I think that that's better…wouldn't you say? Like the factories. All of these people around us, they consume these goods, and they do not know what they really cost. They think that it costs little money. And that is what matters to them. But they don't know the true cost. We do, and sometimes that prevents us from feeling happy. But would you wish to be ignorant? Would you wish to contribute to pain even un-knowingly?'

'No. I do know that to be true.'

'And so I feel the same about…making love. There are things… I worry, for example, if I am pleasing to you. I worry if I am as enticing as the other women you've been with. But I would also not go back to not understanding the pleasure that can exist between two people.'

'I do not think of other women when I'm with you. It would be an impossible thing. For you are singular, all to yourself.'

She blinked. 'Thank you. I do appreciate that.'

She dressed without waiting for a maid, and the two of them decided to depart without breakfast. They took a curricle, and George drove.

'You must be prepared for the reality that she may not have survived the night.'

Just saying the words made his chest feel heavy.

'I know,' she said. 'I do understand. As I said, I've spent time at the infirmary, visiting children, only to have them be gone when next I've been.'

It would always feel to George as if he were walking to the smouldering wreckage of the factory. Hoping… hoping that there would be a sign of life. Hoping for something that simply wouldn't transpire. But when they arrived, the child was there, sitting up in bed, a bandage on her head.

'Good morning,' he said.

The little girl looked up at him. 'Are you the one who saved me?'

She looked guarded. Angry. He could not blame her. Of all the things he had seen in the world, this child had probably been dealt worse.

Kitty clung to his arm. 'Are you feeling all right?' Kitty asked.

'I don't know,' the girl said. 'This is the nicest bed I've had for a long time.'

'Do you have a family?' George asked.

She shook her head. 'No. I'm on my own. I've been working at a factory and sleeping outside. And last night those men found me. And I know what they were going to do. My mother warned me about them. Before she died. They were the kind of men that got her when she was young. She said you don't ever come back from that.'

She was a child, but she spoke with an edge of weariness and certainty that spoke of having seen many things.

He despised the world that created such a space for her.

'You don't have anywhere to go?'

'I can just go back to where I was.'

'I would rather that you didn't,' he said. 'I should like to take you to a place that I have for children.'

'I'm not an idiot. Fancy men like you, I know what they want.'

'No,' Kitty said. 'George is a good man. The Marquess of Curran, I mean. And I will promise you that you'll be taken care of. It's a school. A school that he wants to send you to. In the country.'

'School?'

'Yes. And my plan is that all of the children who go through there can come out with education, and references.'

'And who pays for it?'

'I do.'

'Why?' she asked.

'Because I had a sister,' he said. 'She was a bastard. You know what that means.'

She nodded. 'Me too. My father is probably someone like you. Might even be you.'

'It isn't,' he said, 'if that helps. But my father is a duke, and he had a little girl. With a woman who was not my mother. My half-sister worked in a factory. And she died. I couldn't help her. But I would like very much to help you.'

And suddenly, she started to weep. Great piteous tears that reached down into a part of George he did not wish to have touched. 'But nobody really wants to help.'

'I do,' he said.

'We do,' Kitty said, touching her arm. 'We want to help you.'

Her eyes met his, luminous and dewy. 'My name is Hazel.'

'Well, Hazel. When the doctor is confident that you are well, we will have a place for you.'

Chapter Twenty-Four

It was the first time that George and Kitty had attended a ball together, most importantly the first time since he had confessed the truth to her of who he was. They had barely had a moment to speak, their morning consumed with checking in on Hazel, and getting arrangements made for her to be sent out to the countryside.

And now, they were in the carriage, whisking through the London night, headed to yet another party.

'This will be strange,' Kitty said.

'As strange as it ever is.'

He looked at the lovely, pale column of her throat. She had never been more beautiful to him.

This growing obsession with his wife was…it was not what he wanted, and after the way that she had helped with Hazel, the way that she had accepted the truth of everything…as if he had thought she wouldn't. The issue with Kitty would be keeping her separate from everything. She would obsess about it. She would wish to be part of it. She would wish to help. And the problem of that was that things happened like what had occurred the other night. It was a violent business. It was a tragic business.

And he knew that Kitty thought that he should take up his cause in politics. But then…who would deal with the day-to-day? Who would do something? It was the thing that angered him the most. That with all this money and power and immunity, the blue bloods never did anything.

They arrived, and were introduced, and all eyes were upon them. They were, of course, a scandalous sensation among the *ton*. An odd couple, to all who cared to wonder about them. Kitty, so concerned, and George so careless.

Of course, they had no real idea.

They made their way through the room, and all eyes were most definitely upon them.

Kitty drew closer to him. He knew that she did not like that.

'This is normally where I would find a corner.'

'I'm happy to stand in one with you.'

'I don't wish to… Why is it that we are here?'

'Because it is expected. Because when it comes down to it, I do what is expected.'

He wondered if that was really the truth of it. Did he do what was expected because in the end he was attempting to court his father's favour while behind the scenes he dismantled everything? Did he truly care much more about the old man's favour than he would like to admit? He wondered. Truly, he did.

They ended up in a circle of people, and Kitty was on edge, he could feel it.

'Perhaps, you should regale us with a moral lesson,' said the Earl of Wainscott, who frankly, was starting to get on George's nerves.

'And what sort of moral lesson do you suppose you are in need of learning?' Kitty asked.

He had to laugh, because now she had a bit more of that ballroom wit attached to her barbs. In his mind, she had always been quick, but she was adapting. She would certainly regale them with a moral lesson if they so wished, but now she was playing the game a bit more clearly.

He felt a moment of guilt for that. Had he not been the one to tell her that she ought to cultivate a mask?

'I don't know, Kitty, I feel that you know more about the morality of the *ton* than any of us.'

'You know, cynicism is not a virtue, Wainscott,' Kitty said. 'And I fear very much that you think it is. I think that whatever lesson I try to give you will fall upon deaf ears, and we will all find it to be a waste of time.'

George couldn't help but smile at that.

'I see you've given her comprehensive lessons, Curran,' Wainscott said.

'Oh, lessons were not needed. My wife possesses a sharp tongue. And I benefit from it in a number of places.'

Kitty's cheeks coloured.

'It is odd,' Wainscott said. 'The two of you. Given that Kitty has never met a cause she could not champion, and George has never met a cause he could not avoid. Unless of course that cause is whores. And then you champion it quite nicely. So I've been told.'

'I believe we passed each other in the same brothels,' George said. 'And my wife is well aware of my past, so any attempts to bring it up to embarrass me will not work. Anyway, as you all know, I am shameless.'

He could sense Kitty's discomfort. But she knew how this went. It was important that his façade maintained its believability.

'I might've seen you there recently.'

'Now, you and I both know you did not. And my wife knows, as I have been keeping her occupied at home.'

It was a line to all of this. One he would not cross, and that was intimating that he was not faithful to Kitty.

He could see that Kitty felt rather thrown in the deep end at this sort of socialising. She was not long ago a debutante, spared from crude talk.

'You never did mind sharing your particular favourite ladies,' the Earl of Cavendish said. 'Does the same go for your wife?'

'Have a care, Cavendish,' George said. 'I have an impeccable reputation for not caring about a single thing enough to duel over it, but I do not think you wish to test that.'

He knew that the Earl was not smart enough to sense the danger beneath the words, but it was very real. George was not bluffing.

'I dare say, as much as I do not wish to duel you, Marquess, you are not known for being a quick draw. Likely too hung over from the night before.'

'And you are known for being too quick to draw,' George returned.

The other man laughed. Kitty, meanwhile, looked upset.

'If you will excuse us,' he said. 'I think my wife wishes to dance.'

'Your wife is not known for being a dancer,' Cavendish said.

'No. But it speaks to how bored she is standing here speaking to you.'

'I sense you did not care for that,' George said once they were alone.

'It's awful,' Kitty said. 'You're not like them. We are not…we are not like them. Why must we pretend as if this is amusing in any fashion? I can't…I can't stomach it, George, what they think of you. You're a better man than this. You're smarter than this. You're not… cynical. You're not silly. Why do you let them think that you are?'

'We've been over this.'

'Yes. But knowing what I do, and having to come here and see you like this…it makes no earthly sense.'

'It is the way of it.'

'Why?'

She walked away from him, down the hall. And he saw her dart out on to a terrace. Reminiscent of the terrace that they had spoken on that night. That night when he had smoked a cheroot, and he had found himself wanting to tell her everything. That night when he'd realised that the esteem of Kitty Fitzroy meant more to him than nearly anything else.

And yet, he did not have her esteem now.

The terrace was dark, and there was a staircase that wound down towards the garden. 'Leading me down the garden path?'

'Don't,' she said. 'None of this is a joke to me, George. You are not a joke.'

'I know that I'm not,' he said, reaching out and grabbing her arm. 'I know who I am. I don't need them to know.'

'How can you live like this? What is the point of attending these things? Why can we not be who we are? Yes, we will lose friends. Yes—'

'And I will lose the ability to do my work as effectively as I would like.'

'Why? Because if you were a known enemy they could stop you? Nobody could stop you, George. And if you took that weight of yours, and you let them see it combined with your passion, if you took all of this to Parliament…'

'Kitty…'

'Anyone can run around in the dark sabotaging machinery, George. Not just anybody has a seat in the House of Lords waiting for them. You have a political duty as a Claremont.'

'I would be in opposition to my father. Directly.'

'Yes. Does that scare you?'

'Nothing scares me,' he said.

'Perhaps not, but something still has the power to hurt you, whatever you might think.'

She walked away from him, down the stairs, down into the darkness of the night. And he followed.

'Kitty…'

'At least here you're you. At least here I recognise you.'

'You knew who I was when we married.'

'No. I know who you are now. Just as I know who I am now. Much more than I ever have. George…George, these last few days…they have not changed my feelings for you, rather they have made them real. I did not know that you and I were of one accord, I did not know that we believed the same things, cared for the same things, and yet my heart was yours all the same. And it has been the most frightening, terrifying thing to come to that conclusion. That I love you, George. That I loved you before I understood why. That I saw something in you before I knew what it was. My heart recognised yours. I have poured myself into causes and knitting and hiding in corners to avoid having my heart engaged in anything, because the last time I loved it was that house in the country. It was my father. And all of that was taken from me, and the very idea of losing that which I loved again was something that I could not bear.

'But you… George, I love you. You have shown me a different dimension of passion. A different part of myself. And you make it not…you make it not all hurt. Because this fire in me would surely consume me. And yet, with us…it burns, but it does not destroy. George, what we are is something brilliant. What we are is something wonderful. All of this hurt…all of this fire, it makes sense when we are together.'

But he was arrested by what she had said. That she loved him. Everything in him violently rejected the idea of love. Everything in him saw love and perceived a threat.

Love.

There had been another girl who had loved him, and he had failed her. He had failed her, and he had not done enough yet to fix it. And he could not bear…he could not bear Kitty's beautiful, innocent face looking up at him and telling him that.

'No,' he said.

'Why?'

'I cannot love you, Kitty. I am broken. The loss of Hannah broke me. I can…I can fight. I can kill. I can hold you, and I can make you feel pleasure, but I cannot love. I cannot do it.'

'No, George, it is another thing you will not do. You will not show your face. You will not expose yourself. And love is all a part of that. I know, I recognise it, because I'm the same. You know what it cost me, to make love to you that first day? I wanted to in the library. When you told me that you wished to put your cock in me, I wanted it then. I wasn't afraid because I was a virgin. I wasn't afraid because I didn't understand. Your kiss had made me understand well enough, and I wanted it. But what I knew was that I would not be able to protect myself.

'I hide, George. It is what I do. I hide behind all of my strident speeches. How do you not see that? Because then I do not have to reveal anything of myself, all I do is reveal my causes. But never my soul. But with you… with you I have found myself. With you I have been able to show myself. George…we are the same. We are both hiding behind what we can do. We are both hiding in the dark and shadows so that we do not have to risk what we might find in the light, but, George, I love you. I love you. And I would…I would give anything and everything for this. I would fight for it as certainly as I would fight for all the other causes. And if I could fix you by knitting you a pair of socks I damn well would.'

He felt broken. Broken at the declaration. Because of course there were no socks. Of course there was no magic set of words. Of course there was no hope. He was…he was damaged. Irrevocably. And Kitty was not. And this was what he had feared. That by marrying her he was bringing her into his darkness. Because for all that Kitty burned with the same fire as he did, she still had some hope. It was hope that made her believe he should join politics. He had no hope about effecting such change. And so he engaged in guerrilla tactics, because that at least he could do. It was work with his hands, and he was willing to risk his life…

But it was the only thing that he could trust. He did not have a hope in humanity that allowed him to en-vision a space where he could make true and lasting change on that level. And he did not have the kind of hope that would allow him to be loved.

'I cannot love you.'

'George…'

'I cannot love anyone. Kitty, I was prepared to marry Helene to get to her father, and she didn't matter to me at all. I'd have bound her to me for ever to destroy her father, and perhaps I'd have destroyed her with him. I didn't care. I have killed men and felt nothing. That's

who I am. No, Kitty. I'm sorry. I can give you my body.
And I can join with you in the pursuit of justice. But I
cannot love you.'

And with that George turned and walked back to the
ball. And he put his mask firmly back in place, because
of all the things he knew, he knew how to do this best.

And when he heard Kitty weeping jaggedly behind
him, he did not turn. Because he could offer her no
help. Not now. He was the problem. There was no way
he could also be her solution.

Chapter Twenty-Five

Kitty made her decision early the next morning. Hazel was going off to George's house in the country. And she had decided that was where she would go too. If she could not have George, if she could not have his love, then she would be of service. She had only just got to a place where she felt as though she could want something for herself. And she had risked her heart. She had risked everything, confessing her love for George.

She stopped by the Duke and Duchess's house and said a tearful goodbye to Annie. And all she could ask was that Annie passed her love along to Hattie. Because she would not be able to have time to see her.

'I had thought that you and George had something real,' Annie said.

'I hoped so too,' Kitty said. 'But…there is no reason to take it hard. I have…I have found a position that I will enjoy.'

'Work?'

'Not really. Just…my charitable pursuits. And you know how much they mean to me.'

Her cousin nodded. 'I do.'

'Be happy for me.'

But she could not be happy for herself.

Hazel brightened when Kitty joined her at the children's hospital, just on the verge of being put in her carriage to be taken to the country house.

'I'm going to stay with you at the school,' Kitty said.

'You are?'

'Yes.'

Hazel took her tiny hand and put it in Kitty's and for the first time, seemed like a little girl.

'It's hard to believe that things will be all right.'

Kitty looked down at her. And this was where causes became personal. This was where you could not just use them as a shield. But she could use the things that she had been through. She could do that.

'I know what it's like to have everything change. And to not know what lies ahead. My mother died when I was little. And then my father when I was sixteen. And I was brought here. I'm from the country. And I didn't understand anything about living in the city.'

'So this move is not so scary to you.'

'Parts of it are,' Kitty said, feeling fragile. 'Parts of it feel frightening and sad. But I am also…I am also happy. Because I…know that some change can be good. And that…sometimes…change is the very thing that you need to find out who you really are.'

She hoped it was true. She really did. Because right now, she felt broken. Right now, she felt as if she were dying. She had been broken before, but it was different. Death was unforgiving, and you could not make a different choice. But she and George... She wondered if she should stay.

But no, she needed to go. Because George was not going to come to these realisations with her.

He was going to have to decide on his own exactly what they would be. If anything. And in the meantime, there was one thing she knew about herself. That she was determined to make a difference. And so she would do that. She would do that always.

George was fairly well familiar with the concept of hell on earth. It was burning factories and an uncaring populace with far too much power who lorded their particular brand of importance over those they deemed beneath them. It was the unfair lines drawn between children. One daughter born to a wife, the other to a mistress.

Yes, he was familiar with that particular heartbreak. He was familiar with grief. But it was this, this unending, shattering sensation in his chest, that was like grief, and so many more things, spun tightly through his body, this unendurable pain. It reminded him of death, but it was also something more.

He hated it. Kitty was gone, and he hated that too. But she had asked him for love, and he had not been able to give it in return. He could not. He would not.

It was like hands around his throat, choking him. Preventing him from being able to breathe. Being able to think. And he was in a rage. A rage of himself, but also...it was why he found himself riding out early the next morning to see his father. It was two hours on horseback to the Warminster duchy, and it was well worth it.

When he arrived, he was ushered inside quickly, and then taken to his father's drawing room. 'I had wondered when you might come, George,' his father said, his tone icy as ever. He disapproved of George broadly. 'News of your marriage has made its way to us.'

'It was not a secret. But of course, after Dorothea ended up married to a Fitzroy, I suppose you couldn't be bothered to witness a second Claremont–Fitzroy union?'

'The girl hardly counts as a Fitzroy. Being that she's from the middle of nowhere. Though that, some might say, is more offensive than her name.'

'I'm not here to talk to you about Kitty,' he said, his voice hard.

'Are you not?'

'No. I am here to speak to you of honour. For I have kept silent on the subject for too long.'

'George, you are a reprobate who has refused to take even the smallest responsibility. I am not certain what you have to say to me of honour.'

'What of bastard children?'

'George,' his father said, his tone flat. 'Are you a man given to piety and purity?'

'I think we both know that I'm not,' George said. 'But I know how to use French letters and how to spill myself into sheets when the matter arises, and should an accident occur, I would have taken responsibility. It is not the existence of a bastard child, or even infidel-

ity that I want to speak to you of, but what became of
her. Hannah. Her name was Hannah. Do you not care?'

His father's face became clouded. 'You know about
Hannah?'

'I bloody well know about Hannah. I went to her. I
was trying to save her. The factory burned to the ground
and there were no survivors. Because you wouldn't support your child. Because she was born on the wrong side
of the sheets. As if the fault was hers and not yours. Yes.
I know about it. I have known. Why do you think I care
so little for your…your kingdom? For all that you hold
dear? It is a farce, Father. And so are you.'

To his surprise, his father did not get angry. To his
surprise, he went pale instead. 'I did not know what to
do with her. It was a mistake. A costly one. I should
never have been unfaithful to your mother, and I knew
that if she discovered it… She is not the kind of woman
who would have borne it. She would not have ignored
it, she would have…she would've punished me bitterly
for it.'

'You passed a punishment on to a child. Your child.'

'It is the way of things,' he said.

'You could have offered her more. You could have
given them a place to stay.'

'Not without exposing myself.'

'And so she died defending your honour, which was
the thing you could not do.'

'I know,' his father shouted, his hand shaking. 'I
know, George. It is the biggest regret of my life. My
greatest shame. But what was I to do? The Claremont
name, the Claremont legacy…'

It was not as if his anger dissolved. For Hannah was still gone, and the man who could have stopped it was right in front of him. It was only that he realised his father was in that same prison they all were. These rules. Rules that were made, and broken, but which still loomed large and acted as bars all the same. Yes, his father was trapped. And he was a fool to believe that these things were more important than life. Than love.

But then George looked at his own self, and he realised that he was no different.

'Father. I'm going to take my place in the House of Lords.'

'That is a good thing.'

'I'm going to vocally oppose child labour. And unfair working conditions in factories. I will be supporting unions.'

'George. You cannot tell me after all this time of being completely politically inactive that you are a radical.'

'I find that I am. I am a radical when it comes to human life. I do not care about protecting men who will never know a day of labour. I will protect those who have no one here to protect them. Like Hannah. I will do it in her name.'

'George, it will bring shame…'

But he was past that. He'd thought he had to keep this in darkness. But that was cowardice. He understood what he'd thought but…Kitty was right. His power was specific, and few men had it.

He would use it, and use it well, and damn the consequences.

'Then let it all fall. For if this is what we have become to avoid public shame…the shame is on us either way. Simply because others do not know does not mean it is absent. The shame is there. I am ashamed of you. It does not matter that you are the Duke of Warminster. You are not a man of honour. Whatever anyone out there thinks. Honour cannot be given from those outside you nor taken from them. Honour is who you are. And I have behaved with none of it. I have been a coward. But now I will fight for what I believe in. And I will do it in the open whether I have your approval or not.'

He was done being the man who operated in the dark. That man sacrificed all manner of morality. Would use people. That man wasn't worthy of Kitty, who was brave and true and real in every sense.

In every room.

In every conversation.

He'd done the best he could, and he had saved children.

But it was time now to break the system. He had the power to do so, and Kitty had made him see that it was what had to be done.

'George…'

'I will see you in Parliament, Father. I imagine we will be opposing one another.'

And then he left, and got on his horse, but he did not head for London. Because this epiphany was unending. Because what he knew now was that he was in a cage of his own making too. One that did not allow him to love for fear of being hurt. For fear of being destroyed as he had been when Hannah had died. What his father did had disappointed him. But it was he…it was he who suffered for these rules. He and Kitty. He would not allow them to suffer any more. Damn the consequences.

He was breaking all the walls down.

And so he rode towards his own country estate as if the hounds of hell were after him.

Chapter Twenty-Six

Kitty had spent a wonderful few days with Hazel. She was a sweet, smart child, and while Kitty loved all the children there, there was a special bond between herself and this girl. If things had been different between herself and George, she might have wanted to take her in. To adopt her. But as it was…it was better for them both that they stayed in the country.

It made her heart break all over again to see this place. This place that her husband had put together out of all the love in his heart that he would not allow himself to feel. And not allow himself to receive.

This entire home was devoted to the children. A boarding school like none other. And they were thriving.

Today she and Hazel were sitting in sunbeams in the sitting room, knitting socks. Hazel had liked the idea of sending something back to the children at the hospital she had been treated at, and Kitty needed something to occupy herself so she didn't fall into a total malaise.

Suddenly, there was a commotion, and she heard the

staff scurrying about. Kitty got up, not paying attention to her yarn ball which—unbeknown to her—became caught on her heel.

She walked out of the sitting room, across the hall and into the kitchen. 'Ladies? Is ought amiss?'

'It's only that…'

She felt a sudden tug at her foot and looked down. She could see now that she had scarlet yarn trailing after her, and out of the kitchen. 'Oh, honestly…'

She opened the door and looked out into the hall. And stopped.

Crouched down, just there, was George Claremont, Marquess of Curran—her husband. And he had her yarn.

He stood, slowly, and he began to turn the yarn ball just so. And Kitty found herself going to him.

She would always go to him.

No matter what.

Always.

They did not speak, rather she simply followed that crimson string. He might as well have held her heart in his hand.

Finally, she stood before him, the end of the yarn clutched tight between her thumb and forefinger, the ball resting in his palm.

'What are you doing here?' she whispered.

'I came for you,' he said.

'George…'

He took her into his arms, and crushed her against him, bringing his head down for a kiss. 'Kitty,' he said, his voice rough. 'I love you.'

'George,' she whispered, letting the yarn drop.

'I went to see my father. I confronted him. And... Kitty, he's ashamed of himself. He cared for Hannah, but these...these rules, they meant more to him. What other people thought meant more to him than the safety of another person—his daughter—and I could see clearly that that was folly. I could see it. And yet, I looked at myself, and realised that I have not been any different. I set rules to protect myself. To keep myself from being hurt. I tried to keep you at a distance. I tried to keep you for sex. I tried to keep you separate from my work. From my heart. But you were my heart, standing there in that ballroom corner...'

'It was an egg,' she said softly.

'What?'

'The ballroom was egg-shaped. There wasn't a corner.'

'You silly woman. You are my heart. Speaking all the things from the depths of my own soul, when I was too afraid to do it.'

She burst into tears, moisture tracking down her cheeks. 'George. You are my heart. The ferocity. The action that I could not take. And more than that...you have allowed me to be more than just a cause. I care very deeply about what is happening in the world. But I realise that I can love as well. That I can have things too. I was using these causes to shield myself. Making them more important than my own feelings, because I didn't...I didn't want to be hurt again either. I didn't want to love only to lose. George. I love you. And you have set me free.'

'No,' he said. 'You have set me free.'

'George. I want you to stay a few days. And see how well the children are doing.'

'I would like that.'

'And then we can go home.'

'We will have to. I'm taking my place in Parliament. And I have a feeling that I'm about to disrupt things.'

'George,' she said. 'That's wonderful. I'm so pleased I…'

'Don't be too pleased. We are likely to be invited to a few more things than we were before.'

'Well, if the topic is politics, then I am all for it.'

'We will then be disinvited directly. Especially once my politics are known.'

'That is also fine with me.'

She looked back towards the sitting room. Towards Hazel. 'George…there's another matter I wish to discuss with you.'

Epilogue

A year later, George had successfully introduced a piece of legislation to Parliament that would ensure better practices in factories, and limit some of the conditions the children were subjected to. It was not as much as he wanted, but it was just the beginning. It was also when Kitty gave birth to their second child. Hazel was, of course, their first. Adopted shortly after they returned to London.

A boy. The future Duke of Warminster.

'He's so cute,' Hazel said, her eyes shining. George looked at her, and he felt a swelling pride in his chest. He would always regret the loss of Hannah. Hazel did not replace her. But Hannah's legacy was all the children that he had saved. Hazel was part of what Hannah's short life had accomplished.

He could only marvel at all the love his half-sister, whom he had not got to know as much as he'd wanted, had introduced to him. Because it was also his path to finding Kitty.

'Who ended up being society's most scandalous last

year?' Kitty suddenly asked, looking up from holding their son.

'What made you think of that?'

'You know. I don't know. I was just thinking about things that mattered…and things that absolutely don't.'

'It may have been Annie. After…'

'Well,' she said, laughing. 'That is true.'

'What shall we name him?' Hazel asked.

'I think we shall name him Edmund,' Kitty said. 'After my father.'

'You know,' George said. 'That is an excellent tribute, Kitty.'

'I had thought my good works would be my tribute to my father, but I realised something recently.'

'What is that?'

'It isn't that. It's love. All of this is because of love.'

George Claremont was no longer society's most scandalous. But he had a feeling he might well be society's most beloved. Because of his wife. Because of his children.

That, he decided, was the very best title of all.

* * * * *

Read on for a teaser from the next instalment of the
Society's Most Scandalous series
How to Survive a Scandal
by Christine Merrill

Annie leaned back into the corner of the carriage, both relieved and mortified by the way things had turned out. Since this William was a member of the Claremont family, they were in no danger at all. But neither had it been necessary for Annie to rush to the rescue of a girl she didn't even particularly like. It was possible that the Captain might have found her and got her home without Annie getting involved at all.

They rode in silence towards the Claremont house, and when they arrived Felicity hopped out of the carriage and rushed up the steps to her house, leaving Annie alone with the Captain.

'Well, Annie,' he said, giving her a wolfish smile. 'Aren't you getting out? This is your home as well, is it not?'

If she wanted to keep her disguise in place, she really should get out here as well, and make some effort to pretend that she was Felicity's maid. But the night had been long, and her feet were tired, and she just wanted to go home without having to explain anything. So she sat there in silence, waiting for the Captain to speak again.

'I thought not,' he said, folding his arms and giving her a critical look. 'You may dress like a maid, but if you are one then I am Arthur Wellesley.'

Then he tapped his stick against the box, to tell the driver to continue driving.

She folded her arms and looked back at him with the same sullen look he was giving her. It hardly seemed fair that a man who had knowingly attended that bacchanal had the right to chastise her for wandering into it by mistake.

His look, which had gone from sullen to expectant, now turned annoyed. 'You express no contrition at all, do you? What guarantee do I have that you will not run right back into trouble when I let go of you?'

'It is not your job to worry about me,' she said.

'But it appears that someone should,' he replied. 'You are running riot about London in the middle of the night with strange men.'

'Are you strange?' she said with a smile. 'Because you seemed normal enough when I asked for your help.'

Love Harlequin romance?

DISCOVER.

Be the first to find out about promotions, news and exclusive content!

 Facebook.com/HarlequinBooks

Twitter.com/HarlequinBooks

Instagram.com/HarlequinBooks

Pinterest.com/HarlequinBooks

YouTube.com/HarlequinBooks

ReaderService.com

EXPLORE.

Sign up for the Harlequin e-newsletter and download a free book from any series at **TryHarlequin.com**

CONNECT.

Join our Harlequin community to share your thoughts and connect with other romance readers!
Facebook.com/groups/HarlequinConnection

HARLEQUIN

Heartfelt or thrilling, passionate or uplifting—Harlequin is more than just happily-ever-after.

With twelve different series to choose from and new books available every month, you are sure to find stories that will move you, uplift you, inspire and delight you.

SIGN UP FOR THE HARLEQUIN NEWSLETTER
Be the first to hear about great new reads and exciting offers!

Harlequin.com/newsletters

HARLEQUIN
PLUS

Announcing a **BRAND-NEW** multimedia subscription service for romance fans like you!

Read, Watch and Play.

Experience the easiest way to get the romance content you crave.

Start your **FREE 7 DAY TRIAL** at <u>www.harlequinplus.com/freetrial</u>.